Killing

Kam

Killing

Kam

The Letters Of Confession Trilogy

A Novel

Gabrielle Jones

Killing Kam

First edition published September 2025

Identifiers:
ISBN: 979-8-9991961-0-1 (Paperback)
ISBN: 979-8-9991961-1-8 (E-book)

For those who have ever been broken. For those who have ever had feelings. And for those who feel they still haven't been heard. Just know, you are loved by someone.

Playlist

Taylor Swift | Labyrinth
Tate McRae | You Broke Me First
Paramore | Crushcrushcrush
Madison Beer | Fools
Tate McRae | Messier
Kelly Clarkson | My Mistake
Sabrina Carpenter | Because I Liked a Boy
Taylor Swift | I Bet You Think About Me
Carly Rae Jepsen | Your Type
Lady Gaga | Paparazzi
Taylor Swift | Down Bad
Conan Gray | Caramel
Tate McRae | Grave
Olivia Rodrigo | Traitor
Gracie Abrams | I Love You, I'm Sorry
Taylor Swift | imgonnagetyouback
Kelly Clarkson | Lighthouse
Anthem Lights | Say Something
DHT | Listen To Your Heart
Olivia Rodrigo | Hope Ur Ok

Prologue

*L*ove. *Love* was a strong feeling she felt that night. The night everything changed for the worst. The night that was filled with misfortune in a way that she could never get back. The way that could make or break a do or die situation in a matter of longing for the revenge she craved to have.

The night a rose grew its thorns, that was once a carnation filled with a lack of love and an ever so tender heart. A carnation, soft and lovely that only wanted to be seen for the way that she felt. Destined for love no matter what it took.

The thought of distinction of two things that were ever so similar, only faded into a fascination that she longed to have escaped, the thought of ever wanting him back into her life. The thought Brielle never wanted to have crossed her mind again in the way it burned in the back of it.

Lipton Devonshire.

Brielle wanted to escape him, truly she did. But no matter what she did, she never could. She never could find a way for the thought of him to escape the topic of every conversation, nor find a way for their past to not haunt her for the mistakes she may have left behind with him.

The sense of closure she lacked to have.

But she never could. She never got the chance, nor did she ever think that she ever would get the chance of meeting his presence again. The night everything changed for the sake of their future.

The night of when killing Kam came to be in the way nobody ever expected to happen.

With tears streaming down her face, she watched Kam Larson walk away with only one intention on his mind. That was to ruin Brielle's life for good, making sure she could never have success or the future she had hoped for.

She had just let him go, just like that. Not only losing the love of her life, Lipton Devonshire that night, but a regret that would fill her mind of letting Kam go so easily. Brielle had another intention to seek her revenge on Kam after that painful night.

A regrettable desire that led to a misfortune that she would have in store for him.

Before Kam came to be on that heart shattering night, there was always a past Brielle looked back to share with her long lost love, Lip. It all started her senior year of high school when she first laid eyes on him, on a day she would never want to forget.

Part One:

The Past

Chapter One

Brielle

*W*hen love blossoms, you treat it like a delicate flower that has just lost all of its petals from being broken. And sometimes you have to take a chance that comes with a small risk to grasp onto that love before it's too late.

Too late that you might regret what you had when it was yours.

Grasping onto the love that roams throughout the halls of high school. Soft, yet tender. Sour, but sweet. Casually cruel in the name of being honest with what your heart craves. Temptation of believing the many things that might hurt you in the long run of it all, no matter what it takes to get there.

Walking the crowded halls, hearing the commotion of the gossip from the short winter break filling the air, to learn that anyone could feed off of anything that was ever said. No matter what anyone did, no matter how *anyone* looked, there would always be drama that filled the halls of Harrison High that I simply wanted no part of.

I was more of a lay back, do your own kinda thing type of gal, unlike my friends, Stella Monroe and Halle Ricks, who were more outgoing than I was. I had my hobbies I enjoyed, such as tending to my garden of flowers or even taking photographs in my free time for the aesthetic.

I was simply myself, Brielle Johnston and nothing could ever change that. No one could ever change that. *Ever.*

My books, softly placed against my chest to push through it all, hoping to make it to class on time.

First days back were always the worst.

This year wasn't anything to dwell on, other than the fact my English teacher could be a handful sometimes when she wanted to be. Most of the students didn't care for her, partly because she gave out a lot of homework. As for me, I didn't mind Mrs. Bachman one bit. She seemed like a down to earth type of person, and that was my favorite thing about her.

Other than that, my classes didn't seem to be anything to stress about one bit as I continued to count down the days until the end of my senior year.

One-hundred and thirty-three days to be exact, that's if we're counting.

Lightly pushing the door open, entering my fourth hour English class. Mrs. Bachman stood at the front of the class as the remainder of students stood around the edge of the classroom with their books in hand. This only meant one thing. A new seating chart.

"Alright class, when I call your name, take a seat in the assigned spot given," she loudly spoke, approaching the room. Pointing at the desks to fit two students at each, she made her way around the room until it met her satisfaction to approach back to the front to begin the lesson. "These will be your assigned seats for the remainder of the year, get to know those around you and then we'll get started."

Taking a seat at my new desk all alone, placed directly in front of her. I looked around, appearing to be the only person without a deskmate other than a single girl sitting behind me, now looking in my direction with long wavy dirty blonde hair and soft pale skin as she wore a pink flared crop-top with light blue ripped jeans

"Nice to meet you, I'm–" her voice started to softly speak.

The sound of the classroom door quickly shut, appearing to be louder than intended. Standing with a bag slung over his shoulder as Mrs. Bachman made her way to the center of the room to meet the students' gaze. "Mr. Devonshire, you're late."

A light smirk lining his soft lips, nodding to the ground. Brown curly hair brushed over his sun-kissed skin and green eyes until he gently combed it back with his right hand. Standing in a cream colored suit, appearing to be in a rush for something.

"It won't happen again, Mrs. Bachman. Sorry."

She nods once, making her way back up to the front of the classroom. "Take a seat, anywhere is fine."

He nods again, throwing his bag off of his shoulder to place on the ground, taking a seat next to the girl that I still haven't caught the name of. He looks in our direction, beginning to pull his laptop out of his bag.

"The name's Sennedy Marie," she adds, glancing back in my direction.

"Brielle. Brielle Johnston."

The two of us glance over in the boy's direction, hoping to get a word out of him other than the occasional sound of him clearing his throat. But there's something about him that I just can't put my finger on. He feels ever so familiar to me, like I should know his name from somewhere, other than the fact that we have been going to school with each other for nearly our whole life.

It's not until his eyes lock with mine that it all comes back to me of who he is. His voice speaks loudly, feeling cocky, but yet with a bit of self-centeredness that comes with it. "Lip Devonshire."

His name rolls off of his tongue, just like he's said it many times before. One that seems ever so familiar, but yet he appears to be someone I want to learn more about and get to know better.

Lipton Devonshire, captain of the high school basketball team. Son of the wealthiest family in town, and future owner of his family's country club. He was a man with his ego set so high that nobody could ever reach, nor even tear down.

My attention turned back to Sennedy, watching her blue eyes never leave Lip's presence. There was something in the way the two looked at each other. A look that possessed both of their faces to show a slight soft smile, watching a blush rise on Sennedy's pale cheeks.

The bell quickly rang, marking the end of fourth period as Mrs. Bachman finished off her lesson plan on the topic of *how to write a perfect essay*. I picked up my books, along with my notecards to get ready for the rest of my classes as I glanced up in Lip's direction to say goodbye for the day.

But he was already gone, almost like he wasn't even there.

"What's your next class, Brielle?" a voice softly asked.

Glancing over, there stood Sennedy as she threw her bag over her shoulder while holding her water bottle in one hand to take a sip.

"AP Government with Mr. Matthews," I sighed, making my way over toward the door. "How about you?"

"Chemistry with Mrs. Walton."

I nod, tugging my books closer to my chest as Sennedy seemed to not want to leave my side while I began to walk the halls. "You seemed pretty interested in the way you looked at Lip back there."

Sennedy rolled her eyes, laughing so only I could hear. "Him and I had a small so-called relationship over the summer while I worked at his family's country club. That was until I found out he went back to dating his ex, Kylie Sanders. After that, I wanted no part of being in a relationship with someone who could be so toxic, but other than that, we still talk on and off. I'll stick to the fictional men I read about in my romance books."

No wonder Lip's ego was set so high. There were other things to base it off of other than the home style life he grew up in. He was dating Kylie Sanders, the cheer captain of our high school with an ego possibly set higher than his.

"Lip doesn't seem like he could be a toxic person. He seems more like a down to earth type of guy."

"The thing is, he isn't a bad guy once you get to know him. It's his friends that make him feel like he has to put on this fake face to be liked by those around, even when he's with Kylie. But once you get to know Lip for the person he is, he's really a sweet guy," she said, coming to a stop in front of her locker. "I should probably let you head off to your class. It was nice meeting you, Brielle."

Sennedy pulls open her locker, leaning down to place her books onto the bottom shelf. My eyes travel their way up to the top of the locker. There sat some textbooks from her other classes next to a copy of *Romeo and Juliet*.

"So you like reading, I take it?" I asked, reaching in to grab the copy of *Romeo and Juliet* out of her locker to glance at the back cover.

"It's one of my favorite things to do."

Nodding to myself, I flip the book back over to the front to see the cover. "Romance is good sometimes, other than when they both die at the end of the novel. It's almost like why did I waste my whole time reading this for the main characters to not even end up together, get what I'm saying?"

"Fair point, but *Romeo* only died in the end for his love to *Juliet* and their relationship had a point with the story behind it. Despite not being able to be together in the end, they still had a story to be told. Same goes for many other romance novels," she laughed, grabbing the book out of my hand.

The bell rang, marking class had started.

Great, I'm late now.

Sennedy slammed her locker, frantic to get her books placed into the right order for her next class. "I really have to get going now, and so do you. I'll see you around!"

Her body pushed past mine, heading off in the direction of her class. Smiling toward her as she walked away, I could tell the two of us were going to be friends from this point forward.

*P*hotography has always been one of my favorite things to do, especially in my free time. Lurking around the quiet gymnasium has always been a safe haven for relieving my inner thoughts for the day.

Plain, calm and relaxed.

Until it wasn't.

"Quite the surprise to see you here," a voice spoke loudly, easing my gaze up toward it. There stood Lip, dressed in a white basketball uniform with a soft smile on his face. "Anything I can help you find?"

"No–" my voice stutters, trying to find my words that suddenly felt lost. "No–first off, it's not really a surprise to see me here at all, it's more of a surprise to see *you* here out of all places. I come here sometimes after school to take photos. Second, there's nothing you can help me with, thank you very much. I was just about to head out."

Brielle, what are you saying?

Lip nods to himself, moving over to the basketball cart next to where I stood. Watching his every movement, like I never wanted to take my eyes off of him. He grabbed a ball and began to dribble it across the court.

"The team captain is always the first one in and the last one to leave. I have to make sure my team is ready for the big game tonight in order for us to have a chance to make it to the spring championship. It could mean a lot to us if we did go that far, especially for the seniors if we win this season. Imagine how many recruiters we'd have-" he rambled on, turning his attention back toward me. "But why am I ranting on about something you could care less about?"

"This seems like it means a lot to you-this whole basketball career you have planned out for yourself. I never realized you were the captain of the team, no wonder why you were dressed up so nicely earlier. That explains a lot."

"You said you were taking photos earlier, can I see them?" he asked, moving in my direction. "You know my hobby now, can't I at least know something about you, Brielle?"

Nodding softly, lifting my camera up to hold in my grasp to flip through the photographs to get a first glance at them as I made my way up next to him. He leaned over my shoulder, tucking the basketball into the crease of his arm.

"I've been taking photography classes for years, it wasn't until recently that I got more into it. That was when I realized that each photo I took had a story behind it. Each image would be described in its own special way to be able to decipher the meaning of life that it has."

"These are amazing–" he sincerely spoke. His attention turns to mine, locking eyes with a slight smile never wanting to leave either one of our faces. "Your talent is special."

Smiling under my breath, pulling my body back to avoid the thought of this person I was getting to know so easily. This Lip seemed like a completely different person from the one I met in class.

One that I could learn to trust with my heart left in his hands.

"I really should get going now–" my voice stuttered, trying to find the correct words. "It was nice talking to you, Lip."

I made my way over toward my stuff on the ground next to the bleachers to tuck my camera into a safe place. Swinging my bag over my shoulder as the sound of a basketball dribbling filled the void of silence.

"Just you and me. One on one. We talk, get to know each other more and play a round of basketball. How does that sound?" his voice spoke, meeting his gaze. The ball held out within my reach.

"It's on, Devonshire."

His smirk grew into a soft smile, watching as our bodies guided across the court. Dribbling the ball in my right hand, continuing my attempt to make a basket while Lip played a strong defense against me.

The sound of rubber repetitively slid against the court, and that's when I realized I had no chance of beating him at his own game. "There's no way you can be that good, you have to be cheating!"

Shooting another basket, to catch the ball for the rebound, he tucked it back underneath the crease of his arm to walk in my direction. "I'm only good because I have to be. Captains don't cheat to get what they want."

A blush rose on my cheeks, turning my pale skin into a bright red. Feeling Lip hovering over me felt more intimidating than ever before. There was something about him that only came out when it was the two of us.

"Aren't you two cute—" a voice spoke, walking in our direction. Turning both of our heads to be met by a boy, who stood a little taller than Lip. Short crisp orange hair brushed back as he guided his hand through it with an innocent smile, wearing the same white uniform. "The name's Otis Hope."

Lip's smile suddenly faded, turning back into that version of him he only seemed to be like when his friends were around. His body guided away from mine, acting as if it was invisible.

Once again, I become nothing to him.

"She was just about to get going. Isn't that right, Brielle?"

"Yeah, and I wish I would have left sooner," I snapped, nudging the side of my shoulder into Lip's body.

"You should stay for the game–" Otis blurted, turning his attention over to mine.

"Otis, she isn't going to stay. Just drop it," Lip cut in with a snap in his tone. "Go start warming up and I'll catch up with you in a minute."

Otis nodded, listening to his captain's demands to start warming up. Lip turned his attention back toward mine, but instead I was already making my way toward the door.

"Brielle, wait!"

Tugging my bag tightly against my shoulder, shaking my head in disbelief. The temptation was strong to leave, but yet I wanted to stand here to listen to what he had to say to plead his case of the person I just watched him become.

This Lipton Devonshire that I knew wasn't truly within him.

"Come to our game next week. I promise it will be worth it."

"But why would I do that? You didn't want me at this game, what makes me think that you'll want me at the next one?"

Sighing under his breath, pulling the emotion down his face to meet my gaze with a strong stare. "Don't do it for *me*. Do it for the school to show your support. Help cheer us on to make it to the championship."

"I'll think about it."

The smile slips from his lips, turning into the captain he needs to be for his team as the sound of cheering and footsteps approach into the gymnasium. Many guys enter, mostly shirtless as others wear the same matching white uniform.

Learning that this is my cue to leave without any explanation and no doubt of what I was getting myself into if I choose to stick around.

Chapter Two

Lipton

*G*et your head in the game, Lipton!

The score was *42-40*, and the clock was running down to nothing. We had practiced all season leading up to this game and we weren't going to walk away losing it like we had in all the years past playing against Lexburg.

We'd win this. I'd make sure of that.

Racing up and down the court with only twenty seconds left on the clock, my heart racing against my chest. Adrenaline flowing through my veins. I've never felt this passionate about anything before.

"Get into formation!" Waving my left hand around to signal my teammates, understanding the play I was about to make as I stood at the top of the key.

Otis, cutting across from the bottom corner to make the other team believe he was about to get the ball to fake the pass instead. Shooting my shot from the top of the key, feeling like the ball was moving in slow motion as the seconds ticked away.

The sweat dripping down my face, watching the anticipation on my teammates faces quickly turning into an ecstatic relief. Watching a three-pointer basket become the deciphering win of it all, while listening to the buzzer go off to mark the end of the game.

Harrison High for the win.

The crowd cheering louder than ever was something I never wanted to get over. My teammates lifting me up with confidence that there wasn't anything greater than a well deserved win after all the hard work we all put into it. And even when there was nothing better than a win, meeting her gorgeous gaze with a well deserved smile.

Standing there, her light brown hair flowing past her shoulders, wearing an oversized black jersey with our team logo on the front and my name on the backside. She was the one who gave me confidence that there was a reason to win every game.

"You did great out there," Kylie's voice whispered, leaning in to kiss my check softly.

Her body guided back, meeting my green eyes that stared into hers. "Are you going to join us for team dinner at Nick's later?"

"That old pizzeria on the other side of town?" she laughed, pulling out her phone to check the time. Nodding once in agreement, watching her eyes flick back to mine. "It's still early, so I don't see why not."

"I'll go tell the team and we'll get finished up here. I'll meet you there."

Smiling softly to myself, turning my back away from her to begin making my way across the court toward the locker room doors to celebrate a much earned win.

*T*he commotion at Nick's was exhilarating and felt never ending. It was a joy to watch my players so upbeat and ecstatic about winning a game they all worked so hard for, especially within a matter of seconds.

"I'd like to take all the credit, thank you very much, but we couldn't have won the game without you, Lip," laughed Otis, taking a sip of his soda. His orange hair ruffled into a mess, wearing khakis with a long sleeve blue shirt. "We really tricked them on that last play."

"We sure did, and this isn't the last time. We have to be ready to face them again in the winter championship in a few weeks." Running my hand through my brown curly hair, nodding to myself. "This is *our* win, not mine. We did this together as a team."

The team went back to mingling in their continued conversations' with one another, to begin eating pizza once it was served. Otis' attention eased up to mine, sitting directly across from where I sat.

"Do you know if Kam is planning on joining us?"

"He texted me earlier asking if we were still planning on meeting at Nick's and I replied back with the time. I have yet to receive a message back. Was he at the game earlier?"

Otis shrugged his shoulders, taking a bite of pizza. "I saw him before practice started and after that I'm unsure of where he went. You know how Kam is, he's here, there, and everywhere when he wants to be."

Kam was one of our best friends. He wasn't on the basketball team like Otis and I were, but we had many of the same interests in the reasons we got along. We had known each other for years and one day Kam just started tagging along to join us in our sport celebrations.

Many never understood why he didn't just join the team if he lurked around so much, but I was one of the many few that knew the reason. Kam struggled with his home life and most of the time he hung out with the team was when he wanted to get away from the place he called home. He didn't want to make a commitment to a team. He just wanted friends who understood his needs and wants, along with desires.

"Does Kam really have to come?" Kylie quietly sighed, so only I could hear. "All he does is just sit around gloating about your success, taking it as his own. He's not even on the team."

Turning in my chair to face her direction, glancing past her shoulder. Speaking of the devil himself as Kam walked in our direction. His golden brown hair combed back, wearing a black shirt with navy blue jeans.

"Ky, he's my friend. It doesn't matter that he's not on the team. We're all here to have a great time and celebrate an even greater win, plus you're not even on the team, so he has as much right to be here as you do."

A laugh slipped past her throat, turning into a side-eye of judgment to glare in my direction, standing up from her chair. "Excuse me, I'll be back in a minute."

"Kylie–" Her arm slipped past my grasp, making her way toward the entrance of the restaurant. Kam took a seat to fill her empty chair, glancing quickly in his direction while maintaining my eyes to not leave Kylie's presence. "Kylie, wait!"

"What's he in a rush for?" Kam's voice muttered, glancing around the table.

Not listening for the replies or making one myself, feeling my feet couldn't stop until they made it to Kylie. This wasn't like her to make me pick sides.

"What has gotten into you?" my voice rose, louder than expected while throwing open the glass door of Nick's. "You make me pick sides, and for what reason?"

Kylie turned around in her path, halfway to the parking lot. Tears streamed down her cheeks with mascara lines to follow, reaching into her bag to grab keys with no hesitation to leave quicker than when she arrived.

"You've always said I'm your good luck charm–but am I really, or am I just some fling to you?" her voice rose, breaking in each word spoken. "When have I ever gone to any of your practices? Never, but there she is taking my spot!"

"Kylie, what are you talking about?"

"You know exactly what I'm talking about, Lipton. It's everywhere, haven't you seen it?" Grabbing her phone out of her pocket, throwing it in my direction. There loaded up to the Harrison High gossip page, a photograph of Brielle and I from practice earlier. *But how could this be?* "Brielle Johnston–her over me? What does she have that I don't?"

"She was in the gym before practice even started, I don't know who took this picture. But it means nothing." I added, handing her phone back. "I'll figure out who took it and have it taken down. It's nothing to worry about, Kylie. I promise."

Yanking the phone out of my hand with a huff in her voice to follow, glaring in my direction that the problem wasn't quite fixed on her end. "I don't want her going anywhere near you anymore."

"Ky–Kylie, I can't control that–"

"Yes–Yes, you can, Lip. Don't be her friend. Be her *enemy*. Make her hate you before she falls in love with you. Make her someone you want to despise, no matter what it takes to make or break her if you want *us* to happen."

"It can't happen like that. You can't force me to pick sides!" I yelled, walking in her direction to grasp onto what I felt I had left of who I knew she was and not who she wanted to be from this point forward. "What am I supposed to do, ignore her?"

"Exactly. If you want to keep me, you forget you ever knew her. Forget about the moment's you've shared and act like she's nothing to you. Be the person I want *you* to be for there to be an *us*."

Shaking my head in disbelief to myself. This wasn't who I wanted to be. I wasn't someone who could be controlled, but yet having someone like Kylie was exactly what that was. Someone who always made me believe they knew what was best for me, no matter what sacrifices I had to make to keep myself from not losing her.

"I can't do that–"

"Then it's over, Lip. If you can't be committed to me a hundred percent, then we're done," her voice broke, wiping the back of her hand against her cheek. "When you can prove she's nothing to you, then come back to me. You better hope you're not too late, because I'm not the type of girl who waits for a man to crawl back to her when it's convenient."

"We can fix this, Ky–"

"No–No we can't. We need a break from each other to figure out our differences. I'll see you around," her voice quivered, turning her body around to leave me alone in silence.

So this was how it was.

This was how it was meant to be.

Broken. Lost without my good luck charm. Clueless of what to do and who I was to become without her.

Becoming this person who I was meant to be for the one I craved to keep in my grasp and to become this person that I was afraid of becoming more like if I chose to stick around. Wanting to hold on, but yet wanting to let go of something that was so familiar.

To better myself, meant becoming someone who I was not deep down inside. But instead becoming the person that everyone wanted me to be if it meant having back the one thing I never wanted to lose.

Chapter Three

Kam

"*I* can't do that–" Otis' voice stuttered, glancing through the door of the gymnasium and back in my direction. "Kam, you do it if you want it so bad."

Glaring over in her direction, standing with long red hair stood Brielle Johnston.

God I couldn't stand her with him.

Don't get me wrong, I loved Brielle for the most part, really I did, but not when it came to the thought of her being in Lip's life. That was something I couldn't stand.

"Does it look like I care?" my voice scoffed, rolling my eyes while also shaking my head in Otis' direction. "Take the damn photo, Otis. Now before it's too late."

"You better not make me regret this–" Turning his body back around, angling his phone up toward the two to quickly snap a photo. "There, are you satisfied?"

Laughing under my breath, glaring once more in their direction to grab the phone out of Otis' hand to check the photo over.

"Satisfied enough to make Brielle Johnston's life a living hell from this point forward." Sending the photo to myself, feeling that piercing smile never leave my lips.

"But why do this, Kam? Brielle didn't do anything wrong, did she?" Otis' voice stutters, glancing over toward the two. "And what about Lip? Won't this ruin his relationship with Ky–"

"You know how I feel about Kylie. She's never liked me and I've never liked her, so what not better than to take away the one thing she still has left. Once everyone sees this photo of the two of them, hell's about to break loose."

Taking one last look with no regrets, I lifted my phone up to forward the image to the one place I knew it wouldn't take long to spread the gossip. Our school's gossip news page where all the drama was waiting to happen.

"You also know why I do this–" my voice spoke quietly, turning toward the other way to begin walking. "If I can't have a life filled with happiness, nor joy for that matter, nobody else should be able to. Brielle is all sunshine, and it's time for that to come to an end. Once and for all. She needs to change–"

"But what has she ever done to you, Kam?"

"Otis, that's enough!" my voice cracked, allowing the emotion to not slip away in the moment. "Go get ready for the game and I'll meet you at Nick's later for dinner."

Otis smiled softly without hesitation as he walked past to push open the gymnasium doors toward the locker rooms and not saying another word.

He had no right to stand up for her, not even one bit to give a second to think about doing it for a person like her.

Brielle was different, almost in a way I could never see. She was like a snake that lurked in the shadows that hadn't had the chance to shed its skin yet.

She was unbearable. She was unbreakable. She was unsolvable for the person she appeared to be becoming as she only got closer to Lipton Devonshire, day-by-day and I wouldn't stand for that.

The commotion filled a packed gymnasium of screaming, loud and proud Harrison High students, watching as their team took the lead during the first half of the neck and neck game.

Lip had been telling me for weeks about how much this game meant for the season, and about how they had been practicing to beat Lexburg to help them get one step closer to the Division One championships.

But yet, I never had an interest in watching any of the games, instead I'd stand alone in the hallway outside of the gymnasium to cheer the team on when they headed back to the locker room after a big win.

"I'll be there soon–I promise. Yeah, I know–I said I'd meet you at the coffee shop almost thirty minutes ago. But–yes, I got caught up with my study hall again." Glancing up toward the voice, meeting her tanned skin and hazel eyes behind her glasses. Brown curly hair flowing down in front of her face, walked Stella Monroe in a quick hurry, hanging up her phone.

"What are you in a quick hurry for?"

Her feet came to a halt, scoffing under her breath. Stella's eyes met mine, approaching in her pathway to prevent her from going any further.

"Well if it isn't Kam Larson," her voice scolded, continuing to glance over my presence. "Can't you see I'm in a rush?"

Moving my body closer to hers, timid in the steps she took back to guide herself toward the lockers in the hallway we stood in. Standing slightly over her, easing my hand up along her arm to make its way to touch her chin softly.

"No need for a rush, dear. Take a second to breathe and talk to me. You never do, and it's for that to change, my dear Stella."

Her eyes shifted up to meet mine, something I wanted to get lost in for days. But I never could. Never wanted to have the feeling of loving again, only to be the one hurt at the end of it, no matter what I did to deserve it.

"Now tell me again, why such a rush?" my voice grew colder, easing my hand along the edge of the locker to pin her against it. A smirk piercing my lips, watching the fear in her eyes as they never left mine.

"I'm already late. I was supposed to meet Brielle almost a half hour ago and I can't keep her waiting any longer–"

"Brielle–" A laugh slipping through my lips at the thought of her name crossing my mind. "Brielle, isn't she a sweet girl? I really wish I was able to know more about her, other than the photos posted to form a judgment on."

"What photos?"

Stella pushed her hands against my chest to move away from the locker, standing freely as she had a new thought to ponder in her mind while guiding along the hallway.

"Haven't you seen?" My voice laughed under my breath, inching toward her. "It's all over, Brielle, your best friend didn't even have the guts to tell you she's seeing someone. She's with Lipton Devonshire." Stella shaking her head in disbelief, glancing over her shoulder to meet my endless smirk of chaos. "Otis even told me everyone started calling them Bipton for short. But you didn't hear this from me."

Continuing to shake her head, lost in the thought of her best friend hiding a secret. *One that never quite existed.* Only seemed to make her lack of trust weaken with Brielle, and this was only the start of it.

"Like I said, I really have to get going–" her voice broke, turning her head toward the door to make a swift exit with the many new thoughts that followed.

But like I said, this was only the start of the downfall of Brielle Johnston and I'd be there watching it from the beginning to end.

No regrets. No remorse. And most of all, no care in the world of what it took to get there.

Chapter Four

Brielle

Where was she?

My mind was frantic, wondering where Stella could be. She was supposed to be here nearly an hour ago. Where was she?

"You won't believe what just happened," Stella's voice exhaustingly spoke, approaching the table I sat at. She swung her backpack off of her shoulder, setting it down next to the chair she took a seat in. "Kam Larson *happened*."

The thought of his name coming out of her mouth brought shivers down my spine. Kam wasn't your normal kind of student. He was different, and not in a good kind of way. But yet, there was something that I never could figure out about him.

Kam Larson was a mystery.

"Do tell–" I laughed, pushing my bright red colored hair behind my ear with a light smile. "What did Kam do this time?"

A laugh ripped through her throat. Her eyes pierced through mine like I should know exactly what she was talking about. But I hadn't a clue. "You know, you and Lipton Devonshire? You really weren't going to tell me about that?"

Shaking my head once, stunned as the same laugh spilled through my lips. "Stella, what are you even talking about?"

"I was minding my business, when I was stopped by Kam on my way to come see you. The two of us talked for a while, and he showed me a photo of you and Lipton. I wouldn't have believed it if I hadn't seen it with my own eyes that it was true. You really have something going on with him?"

"Well, you and I both know that Kam is a pathological liar–so what you saw can't be true. Lipton and I have nothing going on and there probably never will be anything. He isn't into girls like me," I softly rolled my eyes, taking a sip of my drink.

"That's not what everyone else thinks–" her voice softly sang in a nervous rhythm. Stella lifted her phone up, placing it in my direction to get a glimpse of a photograph of what appeared to be Lip and I from just a few short hours ago.

Coughing on the remains of my drink out of pure shock, I glanced around the restaurant to make sure nobody was nearby to listen in on our conversation. I lifted a napkin up to wipe my lips gently. "It's nothing, Stella–"

"Brielle, it's something," her voice spoke, cutting me off. "Look at these comments, everyone is fueled by this. You and Lipton have started something, and I'm not sure where it could go if you feed into what everyone is saying about this. The whole school believes you're a couple–"

"But we're not–"

"But you could be–"

"But we're not, and never will be. He doesn't want a relationship with me, plus isn't Lip dating Kylie Sanders?" I cut in with a sharp glare.

"You haven't heard?" she questioned, shaking her head with disbelief. "You caused them to break up–at least that's the rumor going around. Everyone is using the hashtag, *'Bipton is endgame'*. I can totally see this happening if you feed into these rumors of what everyone else is saying about you two being an endgame and is something that you can make happen if you want."

"Stella, you're throwing too much information at me all at the same time."

She laughed, throwing herself back in her chair with a smile of satisfaction. "You like Lipton, don't you?"

The thought really hadn't ever crossed my mind in the past, but recently it's been different with him and I. I finally felt like I had been able to see him for a different person when he was only around me. That Lipton felt genuine and that was someone I wanted to get to know more about.

"As a friend—yes, but nothing more than that!" I laughed, waving my hands defensively.

"But you can have more. You can have what you've always wanted, Brielle. You can have the school life you've always wanted. Don't you want that?"

Sighing lightly to myself. I looked around the restaurant once more to make sure there wasn't anyone I had missed the first look around. I glanced back toward Stella to shake my head at her vision she had of me for the future.

I better not regret this. I better not regret this influence. I better not regret my love that only grew for Lipton Devonshire from this day on.

"Let's make Bipton happen. Let's make Lipton Devonshire more than a friend. Let's make him mine."

Chapter Five

Lipton

"*Y*ou know man, I just don't get it," Otis' voice laughed as he stood behind me. I placed my golf ball down onto the tee, listening to his voice speak as I got into a stance to hit the ball. "I don't understand how Kylie could make you pick sides in the way she did. Nobody should ever have to pick between their best friend, or someone who claims that they're your devoted girlfriend no matter what."

Laughing under my breath, as I hit the golf ball off of the tee. I turned my attention fully onto Otis, who stood in the same country club attire as I did.

"Tell me about it."

It had been two weeks since I last saw Kylie. Two weeks since her outburst at Nick's over an uncalled situation that she took way out of hand. And two weeks since I got to call her mine.

We were done and broken up.

My good luck charm was gone, and ever since then we haven't won a game.

This was all my fault.

"Have you even talked to Kam about what happened? I'm sure he'd understand you taking time away from him, in order for you to get things straightened up with Kylie again," Otis added, stepping up to take his turn in teeing the ball off.

That was another thing I had been dreading to face. Putting myself in the middle of the situation by having to choose between the two of them. There was no way I could pick one over the other. Never in a million years.

They both had a place in my heart for different reasons.

But I could never let either one of them go.

"I have, but he doesn't seem to care much about the entire situation. You and I both know how Kam can be. He'll say he's fine with something, when truly deep down inside he isn't. He holds grudges over everyone about those minor situations that he's not okay with, that he'll never let go and I just don't understand that side of him."

Otis nods, leaning over his golf club to balance himself on. His smile pierced through his lips, nodding to my every word to form an opinion on.

He never knew the side of Kam that I did, nor would he ever know.

Kam was a mystery to him, as he appeared to me most of the time when I never understood what was going on inside of his head.

"I get it, and I don't think we'll ever understand that side of him," Otis' voice trails off, as he turns on his heels to head back toward the golf cart. "I'm going to head out for the evening since it's getting pretty late. Are you coming?"

Glancing around the course, a thought crossed my mind. "I think I'm actually going to head over to the country club dining hall, to check on my parents and grab a bite to eat before I head home. You're free to join if you'd like."

"Thanks for the offer, but I have a lot of school work to catch up on." His attention turned back toward me, tossing the golf cart keys in my direction. "Then if you're heading toward the club, will you take the cart back for me?"

Nodding in agreement, I made my way over to the golf cart to load up our stuff. Otis headed in the direction of the parking lot to leave as I made my way over to the cart return dock, which was right next to the dining hall.

Pulling into the dock, to turn off the ignition, I glanced around to start unloading the cart as there wasn't an attendant in sight, which there should've been.

This country club definitely needed some work done, especially before I took over ownership from my parents within the next few years.

"Got a cart to return?" a joyful voice echoed in the silence. Turning to meet the voice, there stood a younger girl, dirty blonde hair down past her shoulders. Her eyes met mine, shock filling her lips. "Lipton–I didn't expect to see you here."

"Sennedy–" my voice stutters, feeling the slight smile fill my lips. "I didn't realize you still worked here. I thought you had quit–you know, after everything between us last summer."

A summer I would never forget. Never wanted to forget it as each day went by.

It was a memory I couldn't let go of.

The thought of when I was a different person.

"You know I couldn't forget what we shared. You changed me, Lip, and I still think about us. When things were better, and you were happier. I've seen how much Kylie has changed you–"

"Don't–*Don't* remind me," sticking my hand up toward her, turning the other direction with regret of being placed in this situation. "It's in the past, so let's leave it there."

"I wouldn't make you pick like she does. You know how she is—we all know how Kylie Sanders can be!"

"Sennedy, please–"

"Even you know it, Lip. You've known for a long time what she's done to you. She's made you bitter. You used to be fun, outgoing, and carefree. Now you're someone I can't even see, nor get through to," her voice broke, approaching behind me. "I'm not asking for you to come back to me, what I'm asking is that you give someone else a chance to change you for the better. More than I ever could."

My feet came to a halt, listening clearly to the words she spoke. Every word she said was nothing but the truth. The truth I had been long awaiting to face.

After Sennedy and I broke up at the end of last summer, I quickly moved on with my life and shortly after I really connected with Kylie. But what I hadn't wanted to face was how much my life went downhill from there once I became involved with Kylie.

I wasn't the only one who saw it, everyone did and I hated to admit that. I hated seeing the person I become and the person who I was that I feared I would never become again. My life was finally where I wanted it to be and I was afraid of making one wrong mistake to take a toll on it all.

Everything I had worked so hard to have, could all be taken away by making one wrong move.

I couldn't afford that. Couldn't afford to lose the reputation I worked so hard to have.

"What do you mean, give someone else a chance?"

Sennedy placed her hand on my shoulder, glancing deeply into my eyes. A smile pierced through her lips, almost to boost my confidence. "Don't let your ego get to your head. Open your mind to let someone else into your heart. Trust that everything happens for a reason."

Shaking my head, to pull back from her, making my way over toward the door. I glanced over my shoulder to look at her one last time. "You'll never understand–and don't try and argue with me, because I know that you will. I've changed, and I'm never going to get to where I want to be, if I don't keep being this person that everyone knows I've become."

The silence filled the air, only hearing the sound of the door being pulled open as I made my way out of the storage garage, filled with a new emotion I tended to not let get to myself too easily. The emotion of remorse. The feeling of regret, that maybe I could've done something differently so my life wouldn't have ended up this way.

But we'll never know. We'll never be able to change the past of all the mistakes, nor ever take back the things we should've said or done. I would never get the chance to relive my past to change one thing to make a right. I could never go back to become a new version of myself.

Everything that was all in the past never had a chance to be relived or relearned. It was all what people made of it that you could never change from the person you've become at the end of the day.

I would always be the person people wanted me to be, other than the person I desired to be deep down inside. A version of myself that could never outlive the past that it was always formed to become.

Chapter Six

Brielle

*H*e's staring directly at me.

His eyes pierced through my own stare. Never wanting to look away, but desperately trying to avoid this lack of contact that we've rarely shared before.

But he won't look away, nor will I for that matter.

It felt like it was only us, lost in the moment.

"Earth to Brielle-" Stella's voice shouts, to overhear her in the crowd of students that surrounded us. Her hand waves in front of my face to grab my attention. "What's got your mind so caught up this time, that you can't even watch the game, that you begged me to come to?"

Blinking once, twice and then three times to snap myself out of this daydream. One I never wanted to escape.

It had been two weeks.

Two weeks since project Bipton started, and two weeks since I realized the true feelings in the way I felt deep down for Lipton Devonshire.

The feelings I never thought I could have for a man like him and I knew he was going to be mine, no matter what it took.

"He won't look away, Stella–he won't look away!" my voice eagerly said, pointing over toward Lip, sitting courtside with the rest of his team.

"And how could you possibly know that he's looking at you? There's hundreds of other students surrounding us."

She was right, and I was delusional.

He would never look at me the same way that he looked at other girls. I wasn't what they were and I would never be his type.

Glancing around the gymnasium, nodding to myself that maybe she was right. I glanced back in Lip's direction, but this time he's waving with the tips of his fingers.

Waving in my direction. He was looking at me.

"Wave back, Bre. Then he'll know you saw him!" Stella's voice shouts, jumping with joy, feeling the same excitement I felt.

A smile slipping away on my lips, I lift my hand up to wave slightly in his direction.

But he's frozen, shaking his head with disbelief and laughing to himself under his breath as he pulls his hand back to place on his lap like this never meant a thing to him.

This was some kind of game to him to play with my emotions, like they were his heartstrings to control at his convenience.

Lip's attention shifts away from mine, glancing to his left to start talking to Otis. Then his eyes ease back to the body that speaks, sitting behind them on the opposing team's bleachers.

A body sitting with confidence, to join in on the emotionless conversations they shared, sat Kam laughing under his breath with a smirk that filled his lips.

"I guess it wasn't for me–it was nothing," my voice breaks, holding back the tears wanting to slip past. "I'm going to run to the bathroom, and I'll meet up with you later, okay?"

Stella nods once. I slipped past her, making my way down the bleachers toward the court. My eyes never leave Lip, as he makes his way out to play for the team that was ever so miserably losing but wanting to win this game.

The halls were scarce with a lack of people, hearing only the echoes of screams from the gymnasium that followed them. I entered the bathroom near the commons, one that I had hoped would be filled with silence. But instead, I began to hear a mope in someone's voice, weeping in this place they believed to be alone.

A presence of a girl, standing in a Harrison High cheer uniform, braced herself against the sink as she took the back of her hand to wipe away the tears that filled her eyes. Her brown hair tied behind her back as she turned in my direction.

"*Kylie–*" my voice softly speaks, catching myself off guard that I could be this sympathetic to her. My mind begins to wonder what to say next, clueless of what to do in this situation placed with only us. It was clear she didn't like me and I knew I didn't like her, but yet I still cared. "Are you alright?"

A sigh rolls out of her, sniffing the remains of her tears back in. "I could be, but why would you care? Why would you care to ask me if I'm alright when all you've done, Brielle, is make my life a living hell–you've beyond lost it to get to where you're at, and because of you, I have nothing left!" Her voice firm with every word spoken. "So again, ask me, am I alright–"

"Are you–"

"Of course I'm not alright!" she cuts in, lashing out her tone. "You need to leave him alone. Leave Lip behind because you two will never have anything that is

58

worth holding onto. Leave him, Brielle or you'll regret this."

"You really think you can control me?" I question, laughing in disbelievement. "Lip is his own person, and you can't control me, nor can you control him. If you want him that badly, maybe you shouldn't have left him."

Kylie shakes her head, taking the tips of her fingers to push back the loose pieces of hair that fell down onto her face. She allows a smirk to grow on her lips, tilting her head to the side.

"Oh, Brielle, aren't you a sweetheart–but yet, you're so naive and brutally honest that it hurts to admit the same interest that we share," her voice trails off, making her way toward the bathroom door. "Yet, I won't stop you because it's more fun to watch you fall in love, just to have him break your heart in the end, just like he did mine. And when he does, don't say I didn't tell you so. Because when you fall for a man like Lipton, it will hurt more to let go of him, than if you continue to hold onto him."

The bathroom door swings open, watching Kylie make her exit to head back to the gymnasium. I stood there, lost in the words she spoke to know that everything she said was to confuse me with the feelings

I felt, only hoping I would let go of him to allow him to go back to her.

But I couldn't.

I couldn't let go of these feelings that I rarely ever felt, especially for someone like Lip. Knowing that maybe they could get me somewhere if I constantly kept trying. Never giving up despite the rejection I may get along the way.

I couldn't give up on the hope I had.

The sound of the gymnasium buzzer echoed through the walls of the bathroom, meaning the game had finally ended, which meant they had officially lost another game. I made my way out of the bathroom, entering into the commons to see the commotion held within the room.

Many of the students, angry and upset that Harrison had lost its fourth game in a row after having such a successful winning streak. But nobody had a clue of how our school went from the top ranking team, to one of the lowest, especially this close to the Division championships.

I make my way toward the center of the commons to stand with the lurking crowd of people. I glance around the room, hoping to find Stella mixed up in it, but instead my eyes lock with Lipton's presence entering the common's area, dressed in sweats as his team follows behind him to depart from the game.

"Lipton, wait!" my voice calls out, hoping to catch his attention. It does exactly that, turning over his shoulder to lock eyes with mine to begin walking at a faster pace. "Lip, wait up. I need to talk to you!"

My feet raced after his, never wanting to stop. He comes to a halt in front of the office doors, tugging his gym bag tightly against his shoulder. Lip glances spitefully over my appearance, rolling his eyes once as he allows me to speak.

This wasn't him.

"What do you want this time, Brielle?" His voice was harsh in the tone it spoke, aggravated to take time out of his day to be involved with me. "I really need to get going."

Shaking my head slightly, trying to smile in hopes to bring his confidence back. "I'm sorry about your game. I know how much this means to you–"

"And is that all you're going to say? I really have to get going."

"*No*–But I also wanted to say I'm sorry about what happened between you and Kylie. I almost feel like it's my fault–"

"Because it is, and I don't know how you can't see that," he cuts in, still harsh in his tone. His eyes roll

61

once more before continuing on. "I want this to come across as nice as possible, but please don't take this the wrong way. Leave me alone, Brielle."

This wasn't him I thought to myself again. He wouldn't be this cruel, especially to know of the heart he had deep down that he lacked to ever share with anyone. But I saw it once and I won't forget what it meant to me.

"Lip–"

"Brielle, I said it and I mean it. Leave me alone for good, because the more you want me, the less I will want you around. Nothing will change about any of this despite what you say or do. Nothing will ever make me want you in the way you've grown to want me. It's better to walk away now, than to hold onto the feelings you have instead of just letting them go before they hurt you."

He can't be serious. But he was, and I couldn't let him go.

Not that easily.

Letting a sigh out, Lip turns away like our conversation never meant a thing to him. *Like I never meant a thing to him.* He swings the doors open to walk out of the school, acting as if it didn't phase his mind, able to let this all go.

But unlike my mind, I wanted to hold onto this part of him that I thought I could change. This part of him that maybe I was the only one that could see, despite the dark clouds blocking the sun from shining in where it once shined. I thought as long as I kept trying, I could possibly get through to him, no matter what it took, despite the less he wanted me–it would only make me want him more.

Chapter Seven

Kam

*A*nd she's waving at us.

Brielle's red hair stands out in a crowd of people, wanting to be seen. A moth in a flame that burned through the light.

God I couldn't stand her.

And what, all because of the one she craved to have? The one she wanted to be with, despite doing anything to be with Lip. Willing to stand out at any opportunity when the chance was given?

I couldn't stand it.

Brushing my body closer to Lip's, as I eased my hand on his and Otis' shoulders. I knew I wanted to make one thing clear. Making sure Brielle would make a fool of herself, desperate for the attention she lacked to have.

"Will she ever give this a break?" my voice laughs, rolling my eyes at the sight of her. "She clearly wants you, Devonshire."

"So I should wave back?" Lip questions, looking back in my direction.

"It only makes sense," added Otis.

Lip looks down at his hand, that holds his water bottle that he had just taken a sip from. He almost looks confused, but he shakes it off, setting his water bottle down to have an open hand.

"Wave. At. Her," I softly say, easing my body back, pressing my elbows against the back of the bleachers.

Silence is the only thing I hear from him while the ball dribbles in front of us across the court. Our team makes another losing effort to make a basket.

Coach Becker looks furious, slamming his fist onto his clipboard filled with game plans. He turns his head toward us, locking his eyes onto mine.

I wasn't the brightest one in his books, lacking the quality skills that his players had and shared. I was more of an inconvenience to the coach, as he claimed, I took too much time away from his players.

"Larson–" coaches voice firmer than usual, waving his hand to call in the next set of players. "Leave my players alone."

I roll my eyes. He really thinks that I should care? Like hell I did. My body looks around the room, seeing Brielle still waving.

Amateur.

"Wave back, Devonshire," I cut in, leaning in closer to his face. Lip does exactly as I ask, lifting his hand up to wave with the tips of his fingers. "Let the games begin."

Easing back into my seat, I watch the story unfold. The crowd cheering what felt like, louder than ever as Harrison makes a comeback with a basket. Coach begins to signal in a few new players, calling the old ones out.

But Lip stops waving, and so does she. *Interesting*. Lip stands, looking toward Otis with a nod as he also stands to his feet. The two make their way over to coach, entering the game with all intentions of winning this match.

23-56, not really a surprise that they lost. But Lip seemed shocked, thinking he could've done something to change that.

There was no way he could've, yet he wouldn't listen. He took game losses to heart, more than he should've and it wasn't entirely his fault. He believed since he was the captain of the team, the loss was on him and not the team.

"This is all my fault," Lip's voice sighed, dragging the palms of his hands down his face while taking a seat on the locker room bench.

It wasn't, but he believed it was.

"You tried your best, Lip. There's always the next game!" my voice said with confidence, approaching him.

It was worth a shot of winning the next game. That was their last chance of making it to regionals if they wanted a chance at winning, and that meant putting their all into it.

"But we could've tried harder," Otis' voice cuts in, filled with anger, tossing his gym bag onto the ground in front of Lip's feet.

Would've. Could've. Should've.

But they didn't, and there wasn't a point of dwelling on it.

"This is all *my* fault–" Lip says again, shaking his head in disbelief. He stands up, looking around the room at what was left of his team. "I'm just going to call it a night. Are we still going to meet at the country club later?"

Otis and I nod in agreement, watching Lip grab his bag out of his locker then he headed out to the commons.

"We have to follow him–"

"*We*?" Otis laughs under his breath, rolling his eyes. "Kam, you can follow him. My car is on the other side of the school and the commons are out of my way."

My eyes roll, clicking my tongue with the idea of a thought. "We have to follow him—"

"And for what reason exactly, Mister Persistent?"

There was no reason.

"Losing the game wasn't his fault and he needs us to be there to remind him."

"We've been over this before, we both know deep down it wasn't his fault. But it's not worth having an argument with him. We'll see him later, so again, no point in running after him."

"Just this one time, I beg of you, Otis to listen to me," I plead with my hands in a prayer, approaching him.

Otis grabs his bag, tossing it over his shoulder. He turns around, glaring my body up and down, holding his hand outward. "Fine. Lead the way, Larson."

It was just that easy.

Grinning mischievously, turning my body the other way to make my way out of the locker room as Otis follows in my trail. We make our way to the commons, lying my eyes on what I seeked to uncover in this very presence set before us.

Pressing my hand against the cold cement wall, hiding my body out of plain sight as Otis moved behind me, unsure of what was going on.

A devilish smile piercing through my lips, watching the story unfold at my very control.

"Kam, what are we doing?" Otis whispers, pressing his hand onto my shoulder while peeking his head out to look around.

I shake my head, laughing to myself at the thought of how cruel I could be sometimes, and the chance was precisely within a reaching distance.

And there she stood, pleading her case with Lip. Tears lining Brielle's eyes, as if she had a chance of getting through to him. She didn't know him like Otis and I did, and there was no chance he would listen after such a hard loss he had faced.

"Take the photo–" my voice laughs, holding my phone out for Otis to grab.

"Kam, I told you last time was the only time I would do something like that. I can't do it again, especially to cause hurt to someone else. I just can't–"

"Can't and won't are two different choices, and I don't see you doing anything to make me change my mind. Take the photo–"

"I can't," his voice quivered, pushing the phone back. "I can't do that to *my* best friend."

"Then I guess I'll just have to tell everyone of all the horrible things you've done, like taking the first photo you swore you didn't want to take, but yet you did," I laugh, pushing the phone back harder in his direction.

"You can't do this, Kam. You wouldn't–"

"I would," my voice speaks, not showing emotion in it. "Take. The. Photo."

Otis shakes his head, latching onto my phone like he didn't have a choice, of which he didn't in this case. He holds the phone up, snapping a photo of Brielle and Lip without them even realizing it. He hands the phone back, still shaking his head.

"Are you happy?" he scoffs, turning his body around. "I don't like doing this to my friend, making his life a living hell that he can't escape."

"I'll be happy enough for now. Lip is the one who got himself into this situation, so I'm sure he can figure out how to get out of it."

I look over the photo, allowing it to meet my satisfaction as I post it with no regret onto the school drama page, awaiting the drama that would start brewing within the next minutes. I place my phone back into my pocket, turning my back to face Otis.

70

"It's for the best, Otis."

Truly it was.

"But what about, Brielle? What did she do to deserve to be placed in this situation? She was simply just trying to become friends with Lip. That was it."

What didn't Brielle do? She deserved the pain that came with her pleading relationship to Lip. She could never get through to him, and she was meant to suffer in a way she never expected.

"If we continue to stand around here, Lip will be waiting on us," I firmly say, avoiding the interest in his wondering question, as I push my way past him to make an exit toward the doors.

Leaving Otis and his mind behind to wonder what my intentions were, and truly of what it would take to make sure Lip would never fall in love with Brielle, if it was the last thing I did.

Chapter Eight

Lipton

*W*hat has she done to me?

My mind felt twisted, tainted with a love I wanted to escape. But yet, a desire of not wanting to care of what happened to her. She wanted to get into my mind, but I didn't want to let her in. Not willing to let her get into my head more than she already has.

She's messed everything up.

She's messed me up.

"Lip, this isn't your fault. We all know how Coach Becker can be sometimes. He drills those thoughts into your mind to be a better player, and you did try your best. We all did," Otis says, walking up to hand me a beer.

I grab it out of his hand, cracking it open to take a cold refreshing sip as I shake my head. "I know. I'm just so worked up about trying to get our team to regionals, then after that, possibly if we tried hard enough, we could make it to Divisions."

"You think way too much into this shit, Lip," sighed Kam, dragging himself down into his chair as we sat in the middle of the country club banquet hall. "You've worked your ass off this season, more than any player ever has and you've done so much."

I take another sip of my beer, trying to not let the thought bother me.

The game meant so much to me, probably more than they did to any other player. I had to treat each game like it was my last, especially being it was my senior year and with each game, I had to put my all into it if I wanted a shot of having a college recognition.

It was always my dream to follow on with basketball after high school, and if I made the wrong move, one wrong play, I could kiss that dream goodbye like it never meant a thing.

And that was exactly what I was afraid of as each game continued to pass by with failure to follow, each and every time.

"It's just a game," I laugh under my breath, not showing how much this actually means to me. Not showing how much it truly hurts losing and to believe it was all my fault. "Let's talk about something else—"

The room momentarily goes silent to think as we all pull out our phones to catch up on our socials. The feeling of shock fills my chest, and the sound of my jaw dropping fills the void. My eyes blink in disbelief, looking at my screen to see the emotion that ran through Brielle's face, only hours ago.

Another photo of us, posted for everyone to see what wasn't anything but a lie. A rumor that spread like wildfire. Something I wanted to escape, but each time I tried, I only ever seemed to find a dead end.

Who was doing this to me? Who was doing this to us?

"This is ridiculous!" my voice scoffs, holding my phone out for Kam and Otis to see. They both look confused, unsure of why I cared so much. "Her being in my life has ruined so much–"

"Yet those photographs mysteriously keep appearing," coughed Otis while rolling his eyes, and standing up to ponder his thoughts on the topic.

"If you're so worried about these photos, why don't you just stay away from her?" questioned Kam, inching closer in his seat.

Believe me I've wanted to get away from her, but for some reason I just can't.

"She ran after me, and I'm not entirely sure why."

I knew why and I hated to admit it.

Kam scoffs as he sets his beer down to stand. He begins to walk around the banquet hall, making his way over to Otis. "You just have to run faster because the more she wants you, the less you'll want her around. All she is doing is messing up the life you worked so hard to have."

"Kam is right, Lip. I have to agree with him. Brielle isn't the type of girl you'll want to get yourself wrapped up with. Think of what she did to the relationship you had with Kylie, she's only destroyed that. Think of what Brielle could be capable of if you keep her around," added Otis, turning around toward us.

"She'll destroy your life, Lip," laughed Kam, walking back in my direction. "If you want Kylie back, take our advice and run like your life depends on it."

Nodding toward both of them, I lean back in my seat. The thoughts racing through my mind of the doubts that began to fill it. "I think we should call it a night, guys."

"Really, are you sure?" questioned Otis, taking the last sip of his beer. "The night has only just begun."

I drag my hand down my chin, nodding to myself to avoid their glare of judgement because it wasn't like me to shut a party down this early. The two stood in silence, before making their way up toward me to pat my shoulder and follow in a smooth exit.

My body leans forward to press my elbows against my knees, dragging my phone back out into my hand. I open my text conversation to see the name I crave to have and hope to call mine again.

Kylie Sanders

Me: 9:02 P.M.
Hey.
I've been thinking about you.

I hold the text message open, hoping to get a reply. But I only begin to feel hopeless, that everything was meant to happen for a reason and maybe that losing her was for the better.

But who was I kidding?

Losing Kylie was never supposed to happen in the senseless matter that it did. I should've fought harder to hold onto her, but I didn't and I would live with that regret each and every day that I could've done something differently.

I couldn't have lost my good luck charm that easily.

I sigh to myself, sliding my phone back into my pocket as I rise to my feet with my beer bottle in hand to look at the empty chairs surrounding me in the middle of the banquet hall. I begin to feel clueless of what to do, sinking back into my seat at the sound of my text message notification going off.

Kylie Sanders

Me: 9:02 P.M.
Hey.
I've been thinking about you.

Kylie: 9:05 P.M.
I'd be guilty if I wouldn't be
saying the same thing.
Miss me yet?

Me: 9:05 P.M.
A lot more than you realize.

Kylie: 9:05 P.M.
So you've made up your mind?

Me: 9:06 P.M.
Yeah.
I think we should give our
relationship another try.

Kylie: 9:07 P.M.
I've been waiting for you to say that.

I smile at the conversation, feeling like a weight had been lifted off of my shoulders. My good luck charm was finally back and there was no way possible that we could lose the next game of our rematch to Lexburg.

There were only a few more games before we found out if we would make it to Divisions, and I would put my blood, sweat, and tears into it all to make sure that we had no chance of failure this time around.

I'd make sure of that, with no distractions along the way. Not even Brielle Johnston could get into my mind to stop my team from winning, now that I had Kylie back on my side.

Chapter Nine

Brielle

Mrs. Bachman's lectures could never get boring, especially when it came to discussing our college essay assessments.

"Now as a group, you and your team will discuss your long and short term goals that you would like to achieve during your first year of college," her voice spoke, walking around the classroom to distribute papers to each of our desks.

I grab mine out of her hand, looking it over with an idea in mind.

"How about the three of us work together?" I suggested as I turn myself around in my chair to be met with Sennedy's joyful smile and Lip's dreadful expression with an eye roll to follow.

"I love that idea!" her voice eagerly replied, pulling open her laptop.

"And that sounds like an idea I'll surely pass on," scoffed Lip, grabbing his laptop off of the table as he swung his bag over his shoulder to move to the table behind him.

Sennedy goes wide-eyed, confused as I move my chair over to her table. Her and I were both unsure of what was going on with Lip.

"It seems like his ego has gotten the better of him after you know who reconnected back in his life," she laughed under her breath.

I open my laptop, shrugging off the thought of him as I meet her expression. "What do you mean?"

"You haven't heard?" I shake my head, allowing her to continue on. "Rumor has it, he's back together with Kylie. So much for a long break up, when they couldn't even last a month."

And that says everything about the way he was acting. Same old Lip when his ego got the better of him, and when Kylie came into control.

"He shouldn't let his ego get the better of him–" my voice cuts in, shaking my head. "He should've moved on when the chance was given. But instead he goes back to her?"

Sennedy looks as confused as I do, shrugging her shoulders. She opens a document on her laptop to begin typing her essay. "I tried to warn him months ago to leave her, hoping he could have a new start."

"But what about his college career, do you know what he's planning on doing or is Kylie going to ruin that as well?" I questioned. This shouldn't be bothering me, but yet the words come out like I feel I should care when he clearly doesn't feel the same about me. "Where is he going after all this is over?"

"In the past he's always wanted to go to whatever university could offer him a basketball scholarship with a chance at a good career. And so far, nobody has offered him anything."

The moment flashes back in my mind of the day he and I first talked. The day we played basketball together on the court, he had mentioned he wanted to fulfill a career after high school was over. Which was clear he was still holding onto that dream.

"And what if they don't? What if he has nothing that's offered after high school is over?"

Brielle, why do you care so much?

"If they don't, I'm not sure what will happen. He'll probably just go for a basic degree, or he might just not go at all."

I nod to myself, looking back at my laptop to begin typing my essay again. But the thought of Lip's future still trails in my mind, as if I have to know every little detail about his life.

I've never cared this much about wanting to get to know someone. But with Lip, I felt like I had to know every detail, despite what it was and if it would mean anything along the line at some point.

"You could just talk to him. He's still sitting right behind us," added Sennedy, pointing back toward him.

I glance up, wanting to move closer to him. But only feeling like a magnet that wanted to repel, as if opposites didn't attract.

"Hey Lip–" I raise my hand, trying to get his attention, but I'm cut off instead.

"He doesn't want to talk to you, Brielle," a sharp tone says, glaring in my direction with dark green eyes.

JJ Milton. I should've known. His brown hair brushes over his pale face, beginning to laugh under his breath. One of Lip's basketball teammates.

"So take this nicely, Brielle. Leave Lip alone," JJ adds, as he turns over to face Lip, hoping he would add to the lacking conversation.

Please say something Lip. Anything.

I stare at Lip, like my life was depending on him to speak the words I wanted to hear. To have clarity that it wasn't just his friends speaking for him, that he himself would have his own form of judgement toward me.

"Brielle–" his voice finally says. My jaw falls open, grasping onto the words he speaks so softly.

"Listen to my friends, and leave me alone. It's better that way."

Heartbreak. The feeling of becoming heartbroken sweeps over my chest, but I can't shake it off. Not willing to let his words get the best of me, not that easily.

He still wanted me. I knew he did. I saw the person he became when it was only us and nobody around to twist his words into nonsense to please everyone.

He was the Lipton I believed he could be deep down inside.

The bell rang, marking the end of the hour as everyone began to pack up their things. I stood from my seat, not wanting to look away from him. But instead feeling torn away from the person he may become if I didn't stop it from happening.

Lip grabbed his things, swinging his backpack over his shoulder as he followed JJ out of class. Sennedy followed shortly after, leaving me behind to take it all in.

Chapter Ten

Lipton

*S*he just wouldn't leave me alone, would she?

My hands make their way up toward my face, dragging them down as the thought of her became inescapable. I wanted to forget about every conversation spoken, believe me I did. But I just couldn't, nor could I ever find the sense of closure we lacked to have.

There was something about Brielle that wouldn't leave my mind. I wanted to know more about her, maybe even willing to have more of a lacking conversation to learn what she truly wanted with me.

But I just couldn't do it, only afraid it will mess up my relationship with Kylie again. Something that I wouldn't allow to slip away that easily, not letting go of my good luck charm this time around.

Pacing back and forth on the court, wanting to forget it all, I looked up toward the clock on the wall to see there was only ten minutes left before the team would show up for practice. I sighed softly to myself, coming to a halt to let it go before making my way over to the storage closet to grab out our warm-up equipment.

The storage closet door opens, shutting behind as I approach the center of the closet to tug on the light switch string. Dust fills the air, coughing under my breath while looking around the room. It was clear the storage closet was one of the places the janitors lacked to clean.

Two carts of basketballs sit in the corner of the closet, as a bag of colored warm-up jerseys sit on top. I make my way over, continuing to look around the room, feeling the memorabilia that surrounded me.

Many trophies that dated back to the early eighties from past basketball teams, showing when they had a chance to make it to Division One. I stop in my tracks, picking one up to glance at it as a small smile slips past my lips. Looking at these trophies gave me hope that we still had a chance of making our dream a reality.

I softly set it back down onto the shelf, glancing around the closet again, suddenly feeling something was off as the sound of a clearing of someone's throat filled the silence.

Someone else was in here.

"Hello?" I calmly ask, my body turns in the direction of the basketballs.

No reply. Just silence.

I reach out, grabbing onto the two basketball carts with the jerseys to pull them aside toward the door. A shadow of a person quickly shot up, hitting their head on the table they appeared to be hiding under that was hidden behind those carts.

They cover their head, shaking it back and forth. "*Ow*–that hurt."

The voice is calm, soft spoken and very familiar in my mind as they step out of the shadow and into the light. A pale face with her red hair flowing down in front of it to cover her eyes, before pushing it to the side to lock eyes with mine.

Brielle.

She tilts her head to the side, appearing confused as she looks my body up and down, standing in my basketball uniform.

"Are you alright?" I finally say, taking a step closer to her. I reach my hand out for her to grab to step out from the corner. "You hit your head pretty hard it looked like."

Brielle latches onto my hand, stepping over the other team's sports equipment that surrounded us. She continuously looks into my eyes, starstruck to be alone with just me. For there to be an *us* again alone without any watchful eyes.

The two of us step back toward the center of the closet, staring at each other with no words spoken. I wasn't sure what to say, and even clueless of what she was doing in here alone in the first place.

"Let me check and see if you have a concussion," I add, nudging her toward the table behind us to take a seat so she could be level with me. "Just follow what I say."

She takes a seat on the edge of the table, as I reach over to grab a small flashlight off of the table next to her. I shine it toward her eyes, having her follow my finger behind the light to see if there are any signs of a possible concussion.

"Why are you doing this?" her voice softly asks, stopping her eyes from moving to stare directly at me. "Why are you being nice and caring about me?"

"Because that's what I want to do with my life–" I stutter, watching the confused look never leave her face. "I want to be someone who helps people and someone who can understand them for who they are. A therapist is someone who can do that, and that's what I want to be."

"But what about you and Kylie?"

What about me and Kylie?

"What do you mean?"

"Won't you, talking to me, ruin that?" she asks, tilting her head to the side again. "Aren't you afraid that everything I've done will mess up what you've wanted? Having me around only seems to make you upset and I can't seem to understand that, Lip."

I nod slightly, taking in the words she said, glancing back to stare into her eyes. "It's because you will, Brielle. You'll ruin everything I've worked so hard to have. You'll ruin my relationships, the one I hope to continue with Kylie. And most of all, you've already ruined me deep down inside for the person I become when I'm around you." She stares wide-eyed, lost in every word I speak. "I can't help but not want to fall in love with you—only to realize you'll be the death of me if I keep you around."

A silence fills the void, staring at each other to become lost in the thought of the words we spoke. I pull the flashlight back out to hold it in front of her eyes, to continue checking for a concussion. But my thoughts soon got the best of me.

The flashlight slips down my hand, falling down onto the ground. My hand gently touches the side of her face, pushing a strand of her red hair behind her ear. I begin to feel her breath slipping past her lips, as my body inches closer in between her legs, for them to become wrapped around where I stood. Her body scoots back on the table, while her arms fall down onto my shoulders.

My hand pushes her chin up to make sure she never lost sight of mine, staring back at hers. A smile tugging on my lips, telling myself I shouldn't be doing this. But yet, the other part of me knew how badly I craved this.

"Brielle–you've already ruined me."

My lips crash into hers, taking in the taste of what I dreamed heaven would feel like. Never wanting to let it go when I finally had it in possession all to myself, without anyone to know about. Not a care in the world that word would ever get out.

Brielle's lips gently pull back, letting out a slight breath. Her eyes blink slowly. "You–you should probably get back out there."

She was right, and I was wrong for doing this. Especially knowing how much it would hurt Kylie if she found out about any of this.

"Yeah. Yeah, you're right–" I stutter, pulling back to drag my fingers along my lips to wipe the taste of her off of them. "What was I thinking?"

"You weren't–" she interrupts, pulling herself off of the desk, to make her way over to the door.

I turn to face her, holding my hand out to stop her. "Don't–wait, you can't leave that way."

"Why not?"

Why Lip? Oh–because it would only mess everything up if your entire basketball team saw you walking out of a storage closet with Brielle Johnston. A girl you claim to have no feelings whatsoever for, after you fought to get another girl back that you call your girlfriend.

The laughingstock you'd become, Lipton.

"Because you just can't–"

Brielle laughs to herself. "I should've known better. It's about your petty reputation you have to have. An ego set so high that nobody can reach, nor tear down. Typical Lip."

She was right and I hated that a sweet girl like her saw it.

"You can't leave that way, not only because it will mess my life up, it will make yours worse," I said, taking a couple steps toward her. "Those photos of us online, that we both don't have a clue of where they're coming from, imagine how much worse that could get if someone sees us walking out of this closet together. It just can't happen, and we can be the only ones to stop it."

"You really don't know who's posting the photos?" she questions, making her way back toward me. I shake my head in reply, watching another confused look possess her face. "I figured you knew, or at least had an idea of who it could possibly be."

"If I knew, I would've put an end to it a long time ago when it started. Trust me, this hasn't only had a bad impact on your life. It's been the same for me, and it's not getting any better the more this person keeps posting these nonsense photographs."

Brielle nods in agreement, walking past me. She glances over her shoulder. "Then what do you want to do? To get out of here without anyone noticing–"

"You'll have to leave through the ceiling tile vents," I softly say, turning my attention toward her. She places her hands on her hips, shaking her head in disbelief. "It's the only way."

"There has to be something else."

"There isn't–now you better get moving, because if that clock is correct, the game will start any minute now. Which means, Otis will be looking for me and these basketballs and he'll walk right through that door any second now to find us standing here."

Brielle shakes her head to the side, walking over to the edge of the closet to figure out a way to get out, while I make my way over to the door. I grab onto the door handle, attempting to pull it open, but it just wouldn't budge.

We're locked in here. *Great.*

Otis will be opening that door any second now–right?

"You get lost, Devonshire?" Brielle's voice laughs across the room.

I glance over my shoulder, baring my teeth. "Shouldn't you be moving?"

"Trying, but it's not as easy as you made it seem."

I roll my eyes, reaching out to tug on the door handle even stronger. The feeling of it still not wanting to open. This couldn't be happening, especially not tonight on such an important game.

"Great," I whisper to myself, hitting my fist onto the door. Brielle's attention shifted over to mine, in a way I had hoped it hadn't. She looked worried for the sake of the game and what it meant to me.

"What's wrong?" she questions, leaning over the makeshift steps she made to pull herself up.

"We're going to lose and it's all going to be–" I started to say, turning my attention to her, but suddenly the door pushed open and the sound of Brielle falling off of the table filled the room.

Otis stood at the door frame, relief filled his face. "I've been looking for you everywhere. You had us worried sick that we were going to lose!"

My eyes locked with Otis', not suddenly caring about Brielle on the other side of the closet. Not caring to run over and help her after her fall, that was entirely my fault.

"Come on, Lip. We have a game to win!" Otis joyfully added, patting his hand on my shoulder before making his way back onto the court.

A smile tugs on the corner of my lips. This was what I wanted. A team and a goal we had to achieve and there was no turning back. No turning back around to walk right back to the one thing that was holding me down.

The thing that had fallen in my grasp, I only wanted to run away from. She wasn't my good luck charm. She was the one thing I wanted to let go of the second I realized how badly she could hurt me if I kept her around.

She would ruin me in the many ways she already has, and I wouldn't let her.

I wouldn't allow Brielle to be mine. I wouldn't let her tear my life into pieces, more than she already has. She would be the death of me to ruin everything I worked so hard to have.

She just wouldn't. I wouldn't allow it.

Chapter Eleven

Lipton

My heart was racing, filled with adrenaline. We were back to where we were meant to be. On the court, owning the game like it was ours to win. Especially ever since my good luck charm came back, we've been invincible.

We've won every game since and tonight was something the team, nor I couldn't afford to lose.

This game was everything I had hoped for. The game to decipher our fate of the future and what it would mean for each one of us as players. A college career that was on the line, and everything I worked to have all led up to this moment.

I couldn't fail now.

"Get into formation!" my voice yells out, just loud enough for each one of my players to hear.

Everyone races to their spots on the court as my eyes lock with Otis' to pull off our signature move that always tends to score us a few points on the board. The ball tosses in the air, making its way to Otis, quickly getting intercepted by the other team.

The ball begins to dribble down to the other end of court toward the other basket, being thrown up to score the point. Shaking my head, to let it not bother me as I race down to the ball while maintaining my eyes on the scoreboard.

17-34, a lot worse than I expected with so little time left to turn this around. We worked so hard to make it this far, and couldn't lose now.

Not today, Lipton. Not today.

We only had a few more games left that we could be able to lose if we wanted a chance at making it to Divison's, but after today, no matter if we won or lost, we'd make it to regionals since our team has done so well this season.

But then again–I couldn't afford to do so poorly today as my eyes made their way toward the crowd seeing a line of college scouts watching each one of us, me in particular to not make a wrong move.

This was all I wanted leading up to this point, but something was throwing me off to lose by this much. My college career was on the line and I couldn't let it slip away after working this hard for all I've ever wanted.

The ball trails back down to our end of the court, another one of my players has it as we all get into a different formation. I wave my hands around, hoping the ball would be passed in my direction as the seconds on the clock tick away. But instead, the ball makes its way to Otis, shooting it up to make a three point shot at the sound of the buzzer.

We lost–but we still made it onto the next round, despite having such a poor game, that only meant we had one more chance we would be able to lose to be out for the season and not make it to Division's. One last opportunity to make or break it.

That last chance was just a matter of three weeks away to figure out the chances of Division's–

"Hey Lip," Otis' voice calls out, making his way over towards me with the ball in his hand. "Tough loss today, but there's always next season in college–"

Next season? What was he talking about? We were still moving onto the next round despite the loss...right?

"Next season?" I laugh out, glancing around the gymnasium to see the other team beginning to celebrate as the scouts make their way out. "What are you talking about?"

"Lip, we're not moving on. This was our last game to make a difference to move on. We've just lost so much this season. I hate to break it to you, but we can forget about Divisions because we're not even making it to regionals."

This couldn't be, I thought I had calculated it all accurately according to the score books. This just couldn't be true, he had to have been wrong.

My eyes flash over to the college scouts standing at the bottom of the bleachers, knowing this truly was my last first impression to make on them. But one of the scouts attention catches on us, standing underneath the basket to point their finger toward us.

"Mister Otis Hope, we'd like to speak with you for a moment," one of their voices loudly spoke to grab our attention.

Otis turns his head, nodding before turning back in my direction. "Don't take this to heart, Lip, we tried our hardest. You tried your hardest and you were a damn good captain–but most of all, you're an even better friend. So don't let any of this get to you."

I nod, holding a smile that feels faker than ever as I watch Otis make his way over to the scouts. My attention turns to the crowd where my good luck charm normally stood, but Kylie was nowhere to be seen.

My heart instantly sinks with the feeling of regret. Maybe this is why I felt off tonight, what if Kylie was never here in the first place and that's why we lost, because I was giving it my all without my good luck charm.

I couldn't shake this one off, not this time if it maybe true like I hoped it hadn't been as it appeared to be.

"You're not going to believe it!" Otis eagerly announces, making his way back in my direction. "They want me! A full ride scholarship to Harris Hills college to play for them! Can you believe that, Lip?"

Every word he spoke went over my head, only hearing the echoes of the one thing I didn't want to hear. He got a scholarship to the school of *my* dreams, not his, for a career I've always dreamed to have.

He got it, and he wasn't even the captain. He got it because of what I worked him up to become. Otis got the dream that was crushed right before my very own eyes.

"Can you believe that, Lip?" his voice questioned again. My eyes trail back to him, shaking my head to allow him to continue on. "I honestly can't even believe it."

"I'm. Proud. Of. You," I snarled, baring my teeth. "Truly and entirely proud of you, Otis–"

Otis nods, making his way over to the rest of the team before heading into the locker room. I didn't feel like joining them, there was nothing to celebrate or even a team worth holding onto with how much pain I felt.

This was my game. The one I was meant to win.

A sigh rolls out of me, turning my back around to make my way toward the far exit of the gymnasium doors. Thoughts filling my head as I brush past the shadows of a few students along the way. One in particular locked eyes with mine, before I swung the door open to avoid the thought of her as she was the thing that continued to allow me to fail.

It was over. My dreams, crushed.

This was all my fault.

There was nothing left I could do.

My team lost. *I lost.*

It was all my fault.

Chapter Twelve

Brielle

*E*ver since then, his lips gently suppress mine in the soft touch they once held. Never wanting to let the taste of him go as I wanted to hold onto it for another second longer, afraid of falling deeper into this love I couldn't seem to escape, growing stronger day-by-day.

The feeling of becoming more like a flower that was starting to grow its thorns to show a different side of themselves from where they blossomed in the beginning. A rose that was sharper than they realized they could be to hurt those around them.

But I couldn't escape these feelings I had, as I felt I still had a chance to make him realize what we shared just a few short weeks ago. The thought of him only taunting my mind that I never wanted to let go.

He would be mine, no matter what it took. I'd make sure of that.

"It should be close to done, right?" Stella's voice questioned, trailing my mind away from my thoughts. I glance up in her direction while pulling my marker back to stand up to look down at the finished project. "It looks good. It gets the point across, don't you think?"

I tilt my head to the side, shaking in agreement to her. "But will it be enough to get his attention?"

Stella shrugs, walking toward the other side of the room. Tonight was the night of one of the biggest basketball games in Lip's high school career, and I wanted to make sure he'd remember it. So Stella and I were able to convince the art teacher to let us borrow her room for an hour before the game to make an unforgettable sign for Lip.

But this wasn't just any sign, it was one that could also change our relationship into something more than the slight friendship we somewhat shared. In big bold letters the sign read, *'will you go to prom with me, Devonshire?'*

Surrounding the words, there was a drawn out picture of a basketball and his jersey number to make sure he saw it was meant for him.

It was risky asking Lip to prom, since he was technically still dating Kylie. But I felt we really had more of a connection after what happened in the storage closet and it was worth taking that risk if it meant following what my heart was telling me to do.

"This will work. I'm sure of it," I joyfully said with confidence in my voice.

I reached down to grab the poster as Stella followed behind to make our way to the other side of the school toward the gymnasium.

The buzzer went off to mark the end of the last timeout in the fourth quarter as we made our way into the stands with the rest of the students to watch the game. The players began to make their way back onto the court as the scoreboard caught my attention to see how much our team was losing by.

We couldn't lose this. Lip couldn't lose.

"Is that a promposal?" a student behind us gawked under their breath. "Who even does those anymore?"

A sigh let out of my chest, trying to avoid it. It really wasn't common anymore for kids to ask others out to dances. Any more it seemed like dances were about just going with your group of friends than anything else. It just didn't seem common to have a date to a dance, but that wasn't going to stop me, nor ruin my senior prom.

"You've got to be kidding me, Brielle Johnston is asking Stella Monroe to prom–" another student's voice added behind us.

Unbelievable–and this is when I remember exactly why I never went to any sports games.

"Can you guys stop," Stella's harsh tone adds, turning her head back toward them. All the kids do is laugh it off as she turns back to face me to make sure I'm alright.

But the feeling of regret begins to fill my stomach, wondering if this was truly the best idea to come here. The promposal, was it worth possibly making a fool of myself in front of the whole school? Everyone behind us already thought I was asking Stella to the dance–was this really worth it?

"Bre, are you alright?" she asks, placing her hand on my shoulder.

I stare directly in front of me, letting the minutes tick by before I find the courage to respond. The minutes tick away, turning into seconds as the buzzer goes off to end the game.

Harrison High lost–

"I have to go–" I stutter, pushing past the students in front of me to make my way to the end of the bleachers.

I looked around toward the exit of the gymnasium doors to see there stood Sennedy with a few of her friends. We lock eyes and hers move down to see the promposal poster in my hands. I wasn't sure from the distance that we stood if she could make out what it said, but I really didn't care. My eyes flash around the room, looking anywhere for Lip.

The crowds are still packed as my thoughts seem to be anywhere other than where they should be. I wasn't sure what to do, what to say or even what to think–until the sight of him told me exactly what I needed to hear.

Lip's body brushes through the crowd on the court, his face holding anger within as this was truly his last chance at a career he hoped to have. He couldn't take it back. He couldn't change what has already happened, and there was nothing I could do to make any of this better.

He lost. The one thing he wanted to have slipped away from his grasp and he couldn't turn back around to repeat it or change the past as we lived in the present. He failed and had to live with it.

But seeing the way he felt, my eyes flashed back to meet Sennedy's, telling myself deep down the one thing I didn't want to face could be true.

I had feelings more than I realized I could face for a man like Lipton. The feeling of caring on a day like today after seeing the way he felt, knowing it hurt him more than it did me. This was his game, his one last chance. And he failed and he would have to live with that regret for the rest of his life if he chooses to.

The feelings I had would get the best of me, and those feelings told me what was best in the moment as I crumbled up the promposal poster to toss in the trash next to me.

It was better that way—better to not become a burden to him on a day that once meant so much to him.

Better to allow my feelings to break free, but instead to just hold them back inside where they've been hidden since the beginning. Not allowing the flower to blossom quite yet, because its thorns might hurt if they prick too soon.

And in the end, the wrong one may end up getting hurt if they listen to what their heart has always been telling them, only because the more I tend to fall in love, the more it seems you're only slipping away.

Chapter Thirteen

Kam

*E*motion was a strong thing she could have felt, but heartbreak was another. Watching the tears line her eyes, realizing the true feelings she never realized she could feel.

But in a moment, it all turns to sadness and despair.

A smirk piercing through my lips to know I got exactly what I wanted as rejection came to be a sweet thing when it all comes crashing down and you're the cause of it. As Brielle begins to question the one thing her heart was telling her, despite the wandering thoughts in her mind.

I would get what I wanted out of this no matter what it took.

Turning on the heels of my feet, I make my way through the gymnasium, locking eyes with those around me. But one in particular catches my attention, standing at a far distance.

Lip's emotions fill his face, not wanting to be seen, but a part of me understands the pain he feels as he stands to talk to Otis. The two don't focus on anything around them but themselves to not notice me standing a few feet away.

I didn't want to be seen. A shadow lurking in the darkness, but always standing in the light of any crowded room.

My attention turned to the crowd, still walking at a slow rhythm pace to study the room. No wonder they lost, I scoffed to myself to notice the one he claimed to love didn't even show.

His good luck charm wasn't in sight. No Kylie, meant no good luck to win the game as Lip claimed she was, each and every time.

She was everything but good luck–but who am I to judge?

He didn't know Kylie like everyone else did, including me. I hated her with a burning passion, just like I did with everyone else.

There was nothing that could change the hate I felt my entire life. Even though some days Lip thought he could change me for the better, never realizing how broken I was to never be fixed.

My body makes its way into the hallway that heads to the locker rooms. I glance over my shoulder to make sure nobody was following, as I turn the corner to push open the doors to the locker rooms.

Silence fills the air other than the sound of my steps echoing throughout the room as I take a seat on a bench in between the lockers.

It wasn't like any of the players would be coming in here after the game since they didn't win. They all normally tended to leave their stuff in the gymnasium or their regular school lockers.

I sigh, pressing my elbows down onto my knees to run my hands through my hair. It was nice being alone to think on a night like tonight–

"Larson, what are you doing here?" Coach Becker's firm voice speaks, stepping out of his office to stand in front of me.

"Don't call me that–" I sigh again, glancing up toward him while rolling my eyes. "You know why I'm here."

Coach rolls his eyes, almost annoyed by my presence before looking down at the clipboard in his hands to begin writing down something. "I've told you what to do regarding your feelings about everything you've been through, you just don't listen to me."

A laugh slips out of my chest, standing to my feet to glare at him.

"The thing is, *you* can't tell me what to do."

"I can't," he laughs under his breath, meeting my glare. "I still am your dad after all, Kam, if you like it or not."

He *was* my dad. Becoming dead to me after he put me up for adoption at a young age, shaping me into this person he could never put himself into raising.

"We don't share the same last name anymore–" my voice cuts deeper than it should, holding back my tears. "You care more about your stupid team than you ever did for me when I was your son."

"And that's where you're wrong," he sighs, placing his hand on my shoulder before I quickly shake it off. "I cared about you when you were my son, as much as I care about you now. You still come to me for guidance, so it shows that you still care as much as you don't want to admit it."

When Coach Becker started coaching at the high school my freshman year, it didn't take me long to realize the connection he and I shared that no other students saw. I knew he was my father long before the coaching started, but I didn't care to reach out or make an effort to talk to him. I always told myself if he came back into my life at some point, I'd have to accept it and move on if I liked it or not.

But when he and I reconnected my freshman year, we made a promise to each other to not let anyone know of the relationship we shared and from this day, not even Lip or Otis know as I forever want it to stay that way.

Even though he was biologically my father, he still hurt me at a young age and that wasn't something I could let go of easily. I was barely old enough to recall what was going on when he decided it was better to put me up for adoption, in which at that age I didn't have a say so. But shortly after my biological mother was in a car crash, that really made my father realize what his future held from that point forward.

If it meant focusing on himself for the better, then so be it. He didn't care because having a child would just be one more thing holding him back from a brighter future, which led to the adoption process for my darker future without any light.

I'd sit in the system, being taken in and out over the course of the next few years to be placed in many different homes to be raised by multiple different family's. These all tended to not be a good fit on my part. That was until my adoptive parents decided to give me a chance when I was fourteen years old.

That's when I thought at the age of fourteen, I finally had my life back on track to learn I was quite wrong in every way possible.

My adoptive foster parents were only in it for the money, using me to share their last name and to get praise here or there from anyone they could, who thought they had built the perfect family from nothing.

But everything isn't always as perfect as they once may seem. Something that was once broken, tainted by the love that others could never share for one to have. The one thing that was never able to be fixed, shattering into more pieces as each day went by.

I glance over in his direction, rolling my eyes, changing the subject. "Did you talk to the scouts about Lip?"

He nods, turning around to gesture to me to follow him toward his office. I lean against the doorframe as he takes a seat, pulling out a file to place onto his desk, flipping it open to hold up a typed up letter in my direction. "Before I give you an answer about this, talk to me about Brielle Johnston. What do you see in her?"

Confusion crosses my face, holding an eyebrow up. "What do *I* see in her? She's just a girl who's getting on my nerves–"

"It's because you like her, isn't it?" he questions, setting the paper back down onto the desk.

I cough out a laugh, shaking my head at his words. "Like her? Are you crazy?"

"I'm just talking to you, Kam. I've seen the way you've looked at her across the court when you've come to games. But I'm not here to argue."

"It's Lip that likes her. Not me. Not ever–" I hesitate on my words, shaking off the thought of her. "Speaking of Lip, what does the letter say?"

Coach Becker stands up, swinging his bag over his shoulder with the folder in his hand. He makes his way up to the doorframe, handing over the folder with the letter that deciphered Lip's future. His fate was in my hands, and truly it was.

"You asked, and I listened. I want you to have trust in me, so after sending out this, no college in the area will offer him a scholarship to have the career I know he's capable of having. This is all because of what you've asked, Kam."

I nod once, smiling as he moves past to make his way toward the door. He glances back in my direction before exiting as he smiles softly. "One more thing. Happy Birthday, Kam."

He opens the door, leaving me behind. Today was like no other, one year older and another day I wouldn't forget as everything only seems to be falling into the way I wanted. A relationship between Brielle and Lip that was fading away day-by-day and now a college career that was in my control without anyone knowing of what I was truly capable of, despite what it took.

Chapter Fourteen

Brielle

A Month and A Half Later

*T*he lights elegantly glistened throughout the Devonshire country club estate, reflecting off of every girl's sparkling dress. The music played aloud as my body swiftly made my grand entrance, standing in a long teal dress covered with a pattern of tiger lilies, allowing it to pop out as the same shade of my hair that flowed straight down, brushing over my shoulders.

Tonight was like no other. It was my senior prom, and although I may be alone, that didn't stop me from attending a night with such a special meaning.

Stella originally planned to go, but she was quickly filled with regret when Kam asked her to go a little over two weeks ago. She didn't want to be rude and tell him she wasn't interested, so instead she backed out at the last minute, claiming she was too sick to attend.

The thought of Kam asking Stella out seemed to confuse the both of us even more, because he really only started to show an interest in her more once those photos of Lip and I started spreading around like wildfire. And it wasn't until the night that the first photo was posted that Stella really even talked to Kam.

As for my other friend, Halle, who wasn't in attendance either tonight as she was off on a school trip with a few other students to Seattle, to tour some college campuses that couldn't be rescheduled or backed out of at the last minute. When she agreed to go on the trip last fall, the date for prom wasn't even announced yet.

But without them here, it wasn't going to hold me back, or stop me from having an unforgettable time.

I walk at a slow pace across the room to make my way over to a table, watching over my shoulder to see a group of students dancing with no intentions of stopping anytime soon. A smile lifted on my lips, taking a seat while setting my silver clutch bag down in front of me.

My eyes make their way around the room, looking for the one I hope to seek, sooner than later as they strike like a bullseye on a target. Standing in a sparkling red dress, her brown hair curled up over her shoulder, stood Kylie with her arm pressed against Lip's upper shoulder.

The two stand there, matching as Lip wears a black tuxedo with a red dress shirt underneath, talking to what appeared to be Otis and his date.

"Quite the party isn't it, dear?" a voice laughed, taking a seat next to me, grabbing a water glass off of the table to take a sip. My attention turns over, lifting an eyebrow to see Kam sitting there in a black tuxedo with a white undershirt. "Surprised to see me, I take it?"

"I just got here, so I wouldn't know-" I hesitated on my own words, not wanting to look away from him. "What are you doing here–with me?"

He takes the last sip out of the water glass, placing it back down onto the table to begin tapping his fingers along the edge of it. "I honestly don't even know what I'm doing at this dance in the first place. I didn't even want to go after Stella backed out–speaking of her, how's she doing?"

"She's fine."

Kam nods, looking around the room. "It was Lip that convinced me to change my mind about tonight, and I'm glad I did."

"Why's that?" I question, looking around the room to see where he's looking, locking my attention on Lip again. "Speaking of Lip, why aren't you hanging out with them? Aren't they your friends?"

"The reason I'm glad I changed my mind about tonight was because I finally got the chance to talk to you, Brielle."

"About what?"

Kam stands to his feet, holding his hand out in front of me. A smile held on his face when his eyes locked with mine in a way I've never seen before. "Can I have this dance to explain?"

My hand inches toward his, wanting to pull it back as soon as it grasps onto his touch. He pulls my body out of my chair, swaying throughout the room, to stand staring into each other's eyes in the middle of the crowded dance floor.

"Tell me, how much do you like him?" Kam's voice softly speaks, inching closer to close the space between us.

I stare at him, confused as my lips fall open. "Who?"

"You like Lip, don't you?" he questioned, spinning me around with one hand. "Mistake me if I'm wrong, but I'm only asking because just like everyone else, I've seen the photos posted online to form a judgement based off of those. I just figured you liked him."

"And why do you want to know? It's not like you could've posted the photos–"

"I didn't, and why would I?" he scoffs, pulling my body in closer for our lips to be inches apart, feeling his breath against my skin. "I just figured you liked Lip–"

"You're wrong, Kam," I scolded, rolling my eyes not wanting to admit the truth of how I felt about Lip. "Just drop it–we have just a few more weeks left of this, and let's hope whoever is spreading these rumors doesn't ignite the flame to become even stronger before school is over."

He nods, swaying our bodies together in the beat of the music. He glances over his shoulder briefly to get a glance of his friends standing a few feet behind us.

"You asked why I wasn't with my friends, it's because of her–Kylie. If she's around, that means I'm not around. That's why Lip and her broke up a few months ago, it wasn't because of you and those photos. It was because she made him choose between his friends or a relationship."

"Then why did they get back together?" I ask, glancing over his shoulder to look at Kylie, throwing her head back laughing at something Lip said.

"He claims she's his, '*good luck charm*,' but she's far from it," he laughs to himself, spinning me around again.

I nod, taking my eyes away from Kylie to stare directly at Kam again, watching his smile fade away into sorrow. There was something about being placed with just him that made me see him differently from the way I made him up in my mind to be.

He always appeared to be a mystery and a pathological liar sometimes when it came to stretching the truth. But being placed here with just him in a crowded room, made me want to see right through him for being someone different.

"Brielle–" his voice softly spoke so only I could hear, grazing his hand over my cheek to touch it softly with his thumb. "Thank you for actually listening to me, and taking the time to spend with me tonight. It means a lot because–"

His body takes another step closer, forcing the proximity to close as I stare into his eyes not wanting to look away. But deep in my heart, a voice inside is telling me to run with what it knows is best. Kam's lips gently trickle over mine, feeling the soft air flowing out.

"Brielle, I–" his voice trembles, trying to find the right words.

My finger finds his lips, pushing them back to begin shaking my head confused as I take a step back to glance over him. "*Stop*–no, I can't."

Kam opens his eyes, swallowing his nerves back down his throat to look around the room. Regret filling his body, only afraid he would be the next fool involved with me to win over the next title headline on the school's gossip page.

I slowly begin the back up, unsure of what to say as I make my way back over to the table to grab my bag. Kam stays a distance back, turning to face his friends, but his eyes never leave mine, beginning to make my way out of the country club.

There was something about Kam. Something I haven't figured out quite yet. A mystery that needs to be solved to be uncovered. A man that lurked within the shadows with many untold truths. The one that is digging themselves deeper into my mind as the days go by to keep myself wondering why.

Chapter Fifteen

Lipton

She wasn't there, but part of my heart wanted to let that go to believe it was for a reason. The true sense of clarity of why Kylie wasn't at the game that cost my college career. The game I needed her at the most and she wasn't there.

But a month had passed, and my heart eventually let it go to believe that things happen for a reason. I didn't want to hold this over her, afraid it would taint our relationship more to cause an even bigger crack that was already in it.

I couldn't afford to lose her.

"Time to line up for pictures!" a voice yelled out across the room of the country club. "Grab your date and show your best smiles!"

Kylie's body approached mine, turning away from her group of friends. She stood in a long sequined red dress as her brown hair curled up over her shoulder. A smile lingering on her face, staring directly into my eyes.

"You look beautiful." I smile, grabbing ahold of her hand to kiss it gently. A slight eye roll comes from her in return, glancing around the room toward my friends.

"Do we really have to go...with *them*?" she scoffs, brushing her hand down my shoulder.

I glanced over to see my friends standing in a group laughing as they talked to each other. Otis held his arm around his date, who stood in a pink dress. As Kam stood with his hands in his dress pants pockets nodding to anything Otis said with a smile on his face.

Kam's date backed out last minute and I felt bad for him, being it was his senior year prom and this was something that couldn't be made up. I talked to him, to try and convince him to still go, in which he actually listened surprisingly.

He had asked Stella Monroe to go a few weeks back and I only knew who she was because she was best friends with Brielle. It really did shock Otis and I that Kam even had an interest in asking Stella out, since he never talked about her before.

But like any friend, we supported him and told him to take his shot. He asked. She agreed. Then she backed out at the last minute, not even replying to any of his messages or calls.

"Ky, they're my friends," I sighed, pulling her hand along in the direction of them as we began to walk.

Kylie sighed lightly, just enough so I could only hear with probably another eye roll to follow, that I just didn't see. We made our way over to stand with the rest of the group, beginning to pose for photos on the most remarkable and memorable night that nobody would forget.

"*W*here's she going?" I questioned, glancing over Kam's shoulder to watch Brielle making her way out of the banquet hall in a hurry.

Kam turns on the heels of his feet, shrugging his shoulders while tilting his head to the side. He glances over to us, clueless of how to reply as he himself hadn't a clue of why she was in such a hurry to rush out of prom.

"And why exactly do we care?" Kylie's voice entered the conversation, brushing her hand along my shoulder to grab my attention. "Why do *you* care so much?"

Why did I care?

"She's my friend–" I hesitate, coughing out the words I can't seem to find in the way I felt about Brielle. "Someone has to go after her to see if she's alright."

Everyone's heads turn the other direction, glancing around the room to avoid the words I spoke so fondly of. They all suddenly didn't care when it came down to caring about someone else that wasn't themselves.

I glanced over to Kam, watching as his eyes linger around the room at the crowd of people dancing nearby. "You should go after her, Kam."

He coughs out a laugh, shaking his head and rolling his eyes. "*Me*? You're saying I should go after Brielle? Why exactly?"

"You were the one talking to her before she ran off, maybe it was something you said that upset her."

"Well she's *your* friend, Lip–maybe you should go after her if you care so much," Kam laughed, turning his body in our direction to pat his hand on my shoulder.

"Maybe I will–"

"Then if you do, I'm out," Kylie's voice snapped, yanking her hand off of my shoulder to walk in front of me, blocking my view of Kam. "If you care so much about Brielle, then make up your mind,

125

Lipton! I'm done playing these games. You have a choice, it's me or her–"

I look around the room, hoping Brielle may have changed her mind and turned back around to come back. But she didn't. She was gone.

I stare into Kylie's eyes, watching the fire burn right through them in being faced with a decision I had to make. Losing Kylie, or losing Brielle, to never be able to make up for either one of these mistakes, no matter how either one of these ended.

"I'm out!" Kylie's hands held up in the air, admitting defeat as she backed up slowly toward the door before turning around to storm out with rage racing through her body.

"Make up your mind and pick one, Lip," Otis' voice says over my shoulder. I glanced back at him, holding back my emotions that wanted to break free. "It's Kylie or Brielle–make up your mind before it's too late."

I had to make up my mind. But why was I continuing to just stand here not moving my feet?

I had a choice to make that I never wanted to be faced with again, thinking maybe the first time I did make the wrong choice and this was my chance to make that up. I had to pick one over the other, despite what happened and how the situation took place.

I had to follow what my heart was telling me.

My feet raced against the tile of the banquet hall, trying to keep up as I rounded the corner into the hallway to approach the entryway of the building. Kylie's back stood toward me, glancing over her shoulder with a piercing smile lining her lips.

She quickly reaches her hands out, grabbing a hold of a full basket of golf balls that was placed on top of the reception counter for the golfers. She turns toward my presence, beginning to chuck them with full force, making sure when they hit that it would hurt.

"It's always, Brielle this, Brielle that! And guess what, I'm sick of hearing about her!" Kylie's voice yells, throwing a handful of golf balls in my direction as I dodge a few of them.

"Please stop, Kylie. We can talk this out!" my voice pleaded, holding my hands up defensively.

The basket falls to the ground, empty as Kylie glances around the entryway for something else to take her anger out on. Her eyes make their way over to a golf club cross on the wall, with a championship trophy underneath.

"Really, we can talk about this—" Her body passes mine, making her way over toward the golf clubs, yanking one off of the wall without a care to swing over her shoulder. She locks her eyes with mine before making her way over to the door to exit. "Kylie, you don't have to do this. It's all just a misunderstanding!"

The entryway door swings open as I begin to follow Kylie into the parking lot. The golf club still swung over her shoulder, unsure of what her intentions were to do with it. She takes a few steps, turning her attention over to watch me while she walks backwards, beginning to swing the golf club around.

A laugh begins to slip out of her. "You're crazy to think we can make this up, Lipton. To think this is all one big misunderstanding? That's where you're wrong, pretty boy!"

The golf club swings in the air, getting ready to strike its target and that's when I notice the object she's standing before. *My car*–was her target.

"Kylie–" Before I could even get the rest of the sentence out, her first strike was hit, shattering the windshield, watching the shards fly everywhere.

"That girl is psychotic, if she thinks that she can end up with a man like you!" she yells out, swinging the club into the hood of the car, leaving multiple dents. "You're both crazy–maybe you're just a perfect match made in heaven!"

I stand there, watching her destroy one of the many things I have left that I truly cared about and there was nothing I could do to stop her. Nothing I could say, unless I wanted to end up with a golf club to the face.

My voice wanted to speak, unsure if I would say the right thing to please her this time or if she would just do more damage, emotionally or even physically.

The club hits at least another fifteen to twenty times before she comes to a stop, screaming out what was on her mind, each and every time. She throws it to my feet, glancing up in my direction while wiping the sweat off of her forehead.

"We're done—over," she pants out. "Don't call me unless you have something to prove to me that I'm worth it. We're over, Lipton!"

The rattling of the club fills the silence watching Kylie storm away into the unknown. I glance down to my feet, reaching down to clench the club in my fist, filled with only anger running through my veins.

Maybe this was all supposed to happen. Maybe my heart was meant to be broken before it could truly be loved. Maybe Kylie wasn't actually my good luck charm all along and it was all just in my head that I learned to believe it was all what was right for me.

Learning that I had to make the mistakes I never wanted to face in my life, if I wanted to get to where I wanted to be later on in my future.

I clench the club harder in my hand, rising back up to my feet as I stare toward my car, holding back the many emotions I was feeling. With no regrets I threw the club directly through what was left of the windshield.

"Are you alright?" a voice lightly questioned from behind me.

I turned my attention around, nodding to see there stood Kam and Otis with lacking smiles, almost like they saw the whole thing unfold within those few seconds. My emotion fades, approaching them to not show my weakness in the way I felt.

"I know I could use a drink," I laugh, putting my arms around them as we walk back toward the country club for the rest of the evening.

Chapter Sixteen

Kam

*T*he car ride over to Otis' was more relaxing than anything, especially for Lip after the night he had tonight.

I sat in the passenger seat, staring out the window as Otis drove us over to his house after dropping off his date. Lip sat in the backseat, silent with his thoughts trailing through his mind if Kylie would ever come back to him.

We doubted that she would after the way she handled the situation tonight.

In Lip's dad's eyes, he declared the car was totaled and not worth fixing. They had plenty of money to easily buy Lip a new car if he wanted, instead of fixing the one he had. Plus this was the perfect excuse to get a new car with graduation right around the corner.

Otis pulled into his driveway, putting the car in park. He glanced over his shoulder toward the back seat. A smile tugging on his lips. "How does a guy's movie night sound?"

I glanced in Otis' direction then back toward Lip, waiting for someone to answer and say something.

"I guess we could–but I'm not really in the mood to be social," Lip finally said, turning his attention to the car door. "I just can't stop thinking about...her."

Here we go again.

I roll my eyes, glancing over toward the house letting out a light sigh. "Lip it was for the better. Let her go and actually try to enjoy this guy's night Otis suggested."

"Everything happens for a reason," Otis adds, opening his door to get out.

It truly was. Letting Kylie go was what he needed to find the clarity for himself, and just maybe it was for the better that him losing Brielle also came with the price of it all, despite how it all played out.

All the car doors open then shut, making our way up to the house. Otis opens the front door, greeting his parents who are sitting on the couch as we follow behind him to make our way down to his basement.

We threw our stuff down next to the bottom of the steps, while Otis headed over to the television to pick out a movie. Lip and I made our way over to the beanbag chairs to take a seat, watching Otis decipher between *White Chicks* or *Legally Blonde*.

Neither one of them would've been my ideal first choice, nor my second. But the choice was eventually made to watch *White Chicks*.

Otis handed us both a beer and took a seat on the left side of Lip, who sat in the middle, while I sat on the right side of Lip, taking a sip of my beer. The movie started to play, leaning back in the beanbag to relax and try to actually enjoy the movie.

"I'm going to grab some popcorn, does anyone want any?" Otis asks, standing from his beanbag.

The two of us nod, watching Otis leave us behind in silence.

Lip leans forward in his beanbag, pressing his elbows against his knees. He begins tapping his foot in a quick motion.

"Why did you guys come find me?" he hesitates on his own words. "I thought you didn't care–"

I didn't. But Otis did.

"Because you're our best friend and we had to make sure you were alright after everything that happened," I replied, glancing over in his direction.

It was Otis that cared more than anything.

Lip nods. "What happened between you and Brielle–you seemed pretty into her?"

A blush rises on my cheeks, rubbing my hand on the back of my neck. "We just talked–"

"And whatever you said must have upset her," he interrupted, taking a sip of his beer. "You could've told her you're sorry for whatever misunderstanding you must have had."

"There was no misunderstanding about anything. We just talked."

I glance over toward the stairs, hoping Otis would enter just so we could end this conversation. But Lip's mouth keeps moving, trying to get anything he could out of me when it was only us.

"What happened with you and Stella? I never realized you liked her either," he adds, shaking his head. "You never tell me anything anymore like you used to. You know you can trust me, right? I'm still the same guy you trusted all those years ago when we first met."

"I never *liked* Stella, now that ends that discussion–"

"And what about Brielle? You've never talked to her before, and when you've told me about her in the past, you've seemed to hate her. Why the sudden change at prom?"

Can he just shut up please!

I take a sip of my beer, sighing softly to drown the thoughts. "She was alone and I felt bad for her, okay?"

"So you do have a heart," he laughs, nudging his hand into my shoulder. I stare at him, with a flat expression, not amused one bit. "I'm joking. I'm joking!"

"Can we please just stop talking about Brielle, I'm sick of hearing about her!"

Lip rolls his eyes, leaning back in his beanbag to watch the movie. "You're starting to sound a lot like Kylie there–"

I shoot a glare in his direction. I hated when he compared me to her, as he put it, I was the male version of her in a lot of ways. Which I hated being described like her in any sort of way.

"I'm sorry about the break up," I sympathetically say to grab his attention. He looks over toward me, lightly holding a smile. "You'll find the one when the time's right."

"You really are a great friend, Kam."

I nod, turning my attention toward the movie. The sound of the stairs creaking fills the room as Otis enters back into the basement, holding two huge bowls of popcorn.

"Got us some popcorn. Hope you don't mind sharing." He passes one bowl over to me, taking a seat next to Lip as he passes over the other bowl to share with him.

I glance over toward the two of them, holding back the regret building up in the back of my throat in all the secrets I held from them.

I never wanted them to know the real reason I talked to Brielle tonight, as I never wanted to show my weaker side.

And I never wanted to let Lip or Otis know the real reason their college careers were going to happen in the way they were told, in the way I had planned, thanks to my relationship to Coach Becker.

There was always a side of me that I would keep hidden from them. From anyone. And that was something I never wanted to get out, truly of the monster I could be within when it came to getting exactly what I wanted.

We had two weeks left of this. Two weeks left of trying to keep it together for their sake. And I'd make sure none of my deepest and most desirable secrets ever got out.

No matter the cost. No matter what it took.

Chapter Seventeen

Brielle

The school bell rang, hearing the sound of it go off for the last time as each hour ticked away to mark the beginning of class and the end, on the final day of school.

I tug my books to my chest, entering Mrs. Bachman's class to take my seat in my normal spot. Right in front of Sennedy and Lip's table. I glance over my shoulder, a smile lining my lips to be met with Sennedy's presence.

"Where's Lip?" I softly question, glancing around the room, hoping to catch his eye.

He's nowhere to be seen. Nowhere in sight.

Sennedy shrugs her shoulders, grabbing out her phone to text Lip to check in on where he's at. I glance back toward my table, opening my laptop to begin submitting my last minute assignments before the end of the day deadline.

"Brielle–" her voice softly speaks. The bell rings, hearing the door close as class is about to begin. I turn in my seat, watching her set down her phone. "Lip isn't coming to class—"

What—what was she talking about? He had to come to class. It was the last day of school and he had to say goodbye to all of his friends. He had to say goodbye to me—and I had to say it to him.

This couldn't be. She had to be wrong.

"Alright class," Mrs. Bachman's voice interrupts, grabbing everyone's attention. "Being it's the last day, please enjoy it and all that I ask of you, is that you get your work turned into me before three o'clock."

I sink in my chair. The feeling of my heart begins to pound, glancing over toward the door with hope filling my veins that maybe she was just joking and he would walk through them any second now.

One. Two. Three. Four. Five. Six. Seven. Eight.

Nothing—those doors didn't open. He wasn't coming?

I glance up to Sennedy, feeling my eyes getting glassy as the words I want to say won't come out. The hope I felt was beginning to drain, that maybe there was nothing left to hold onto. Nothing left was worth holding onto the faith things could change.

Any second now—

Forty-two. Forty-three. Forty-four. Forty-five. Forty-six.

Nothing.

He wasn't coming. He should've been here by now. He had to come.

"He has to," my voice breaks. "He has to show up. It's the last day of school. He can't just not say goodbye–"

"He's not going to show. He's on the other side of town. There's no chance he would show up before the end of the day. It's just not worth it," she says, glancing up from her phone.

I wasn't worth it.

"But he has to!" I cry. The tears began to slip down my cheeks without control. My emotions racing through my veins with no intention of stopping. "I have to say goodbye–"

I can't let him go.

This can't be real. This *can't* be happening.

Not to me.

"I have to tell him I'm sorry. Sorry for everything he had to go through with me. I feel this is all my fault," my voice pleads, raising it in a higher tone.

Sennedy stares in my direction, clueless of what to say as the bell rings to fill her response, watching her stand up to leave. Unsure of when I would see her again since we didn't plan on attending the same college.

I glance around the room, watching everyone leave. Tears filling my eyes. Emotion becomes clear in the way I've always felt about him. He wasn't coming, and it wasn't worth holding onto that hope that I could get my closure with him.

If I could ever say my goodbye, knowing it would be our last.

There was nothing left I could do. Nothing left I could say. There was nothing to turn back time and hope it was yesterday to have one last chance with him to say the things I should've said.

I never got to tell him the one thing I wanted to say from the very beginning. Never truly getting the chance to tell him I was sorry. Sorry for everything I may have done or said, that I never meant for it to happen in the way it had.

He was gone.

Lip was gone for good and I never got to say goodbye.

Part Two:

Two Years Later

Chapter Eighteen

Brielle

Sometimes you never know when that last moment is going to be. Replaying in the back of your mind that you'll never be able to move past, as you tell yourself as the days go by that you've forgotten about it. But yet, it's the one thing that haunts you and keeps you up at night.

The day that fades into darkness and despair as the years go by. A day I want to not hold so close to my heart anymore, hurting it when the thought of him comes near.

But I simply can't forget it. I can't forget *him*.

The nightmares and the storm clouds fogging my mind, keeping me awake at night to want to forget it as I build up scenarios in my mind of all the what ifs. Thinking I could've done something differently to change the actions and consequences.

But here I am, crying myself to sleep once again.

My body raises up on the mattress, pressing my palms against my face to wipe away the tears. A sigh rolls out of my chest, pulling myself out of bed to make my way over to the desk in my dorm. I pull out my computer, looking at the time to see it's a little past one in the morning.

The video chat sound begins to ring, staring back at myself. My red hair brushed over my shoulders all messed up from my pillow, sitting in my pajamas. The call connects for Stella and Halle to be staring back at me, watching the concern looks fill their faces.

"Is everything alright?" Halle questions, sitting there with her dirty blonde hair pulled back lined with red highlights brushing over her tanned skin, wearing pajamas as well. "It's one o'clock in the morning, Bre."

"I'm with Halle, are you alright? You never call us this late, unless something is bothering you or something happened," Stella adds.

A tear slips from my eye, thinking over the thoughts I can't let go. "I can't get it out of my mind. I think about that day, and the things I could've done differently."

"There was nothing you could've done. He wasn't there," Stella yawns, trying to keep her eyes open.

"I can't let it go," I hesitate, tapping my nails on the desk. "I haven't seen him since then, and in my mind I build up all these what ifs. What if he was there? What if that rumor just never got spread, would we have gotten closer or would it have not even brought us together? There's just so much on my mind that I can't let go–"

"You have to find closure, Bre. You have to move past everything that happened. Lip isn't worth holding onto. He would act like your friend one day, then turn around the next like he didn't care about you. He's not worth taking up the time in your heart or your mind," Halle sighs, leaning her chin into the palm of her hand.

I nod, sighing to try and clear my thoughts that are a burden in the back of my mind. The memory of him only seems to fog back up, waiting there for another day when the storm is ready to brew again.

"He used you when you were convenient and played you like a fool. But yet you still miss him? He treated you terribly, Brielle," said Stella, grabbing my attention.

He didn't exactly treat me like the way any man should've treated a woman. He played his game of who was the best at the time to meet his style, that went along with his ego that was held higher than anyone else's.

Lip never wanted to be seen with me. Acted like I was the plague when it came to getting near him, afraid it would ruin his reputation he claimed to have. Every time he got near, I only wanted to get closer each and every time, knowing the price that came with it.

The rumors that spread like wildfire, that to this day we still hadn't a clue of who spread them. Nobody ever stepped up to take the blame and when they shortly stopped after graduation, nobody seemed to care anymore.

I still did, and wanted to know who did it. Wanted to know who had it out for us to make our high school lives a living hell to be controlled at their grasp until it was over.

"I know. But I know he has a different, softer side of him that you guys have never seen. He can be nice."

"We all saw how Kylie changed him, and now he's single to figure out his life on his own. Maybe he can finally drop his alter ego and grow up," sighed Stella.

I nod, yawning at her words. "What even happened with Kylie? I haven't heard about her since high school."

Halle joins the yawning. "She's definitely not what she was in high school. Her ego dropped quickly when all her friends left after they realized how mean she could be to get what she wanted. Everyone just got fed up with her and I can understand why."

Stella nods. "I've heard she's working somewhere on the outskirts of campus. But not entirely sure if that's true, it could just be a rumor."

Shortly after high school ended, everyone went their separate ways. I didn't care much about following the news of what everyone was up to, especially Kylie, as she could be the least of my worries since she broke up with Lip.

Kylie became nothing. *Nothing* to no one. The way it was always meant to be.

"Forget Kylie," I laugh under my breath, rolling my eyes. "She isn't worth our time of this conversation–"

"But Lip is?" interrupts Halle, coughing out his name like it was a pain in the back of her throat. "You can't forget him–he meant the world to you in high school after you realized your true feelings for him. But after everything he allowed to happen, treating you like you were nothing–treating you exactly like the nothing Kylie became. We just don't understand your feelings of why you can't let him go."

I can't either. But part of me still allowed myself to hold onto the memories we shared, making myself believe they were all true and meaningful. That

Lip would never hurt me—more than he maybe already has in my friends eyes.

"How about you write him a letter to tell him how you feel?" suggested Stella eagerly, trying to bring the mood back into the conversation.

She had a valid point, if it meant writing a letter to give to him or even just burning it up, but still getting my emotions onto the paper. It might just be worth giving it a shot.

"You could leave it in his gas tank so when he goes to get gas, he would see it then—or you could just give it to him in person. I mean whatever is easiest and less embarrassing if all else fails to tell him your feelings and to have closure," added Halle.

"I wouldn't even know where to start. I wouldn't know what I would want to say to him. It's been two years. Two years too long," I sigh, pulling my hands down my face.

The girl's sigh, hoping to find the right words to say to add to the conversation. Neither one of them knew how my emotions worked when it came to the way I felt about Lip, and it was probably something neither one of them could come to understand.

"How about you take this time to think of what you want to say, Bre. Write down some notes, reflect on it and then piece it all together. Get your emotions out like your life is depending on it," yawned Halle, brushing her hair back behind her ear. "We could even all get together one night to help come up with the right words to say."

"Like a girl's night?" interrupted Stella. She loved having a girl's night at any chance there was to make one happen. "We could go do karaoke or even go bowling–isn't there a karaoke bar on the other side of town right next to a bowling alley?"

"A girl's night would be perfect actually," I sigh, feeling the smile tugging on my lips.

It wasn't common anymore that I saw the girls since we all went to different colleges. It was a rare occasion that we ever got the chance to hangout. But when we did, we treated it like none other and we always had the best time.

"So are we all down to meet for karaoke next Friday?" questioned Halle, smiling at the thought of it. Stella and I nod. "And Brielle, don't forget to think about your letter. If you want to tell Lip how you feel, this is the way to do so."

I nod again, listening to her words as we all say goodnight for the call to end. I close my laptop, sitting there for the moonlight to be the only thing shining in the dark. My heart pounding in my chest, feeling my breathing tense before thinking about Lip again.

There was something about him I couldn't forget. Something that I didn't want to let go. Not having the sense of closure I lacked to have on the day that replays in my mind. Thinking of all the things I could have done differently. All the things I could've said to have changed his mind back then to make the right choice before it was too late.

The one thing I regretted holding onto, and losing without a chance to know it was no good for me while I still had a chance.

Losing Lip hurt a lot more than I wanted to realize, and there was possibly one more thing I could do before I entirely lost him forever.

Chapter Nineteen

Lipton

*T*he sudden noise of the door opening, jolted my body awake, sitting upright in my bed to face the direction of the sound to make sure everything was alright.

Kam entered, holding our dorm room key in his hand as he glanced over in the direction of Otis sleeping on the other side of the room. He shook his head before taking a seat at my desk, avoiding my presence.

I turned my body to look at the clock to see the time was a little after eight in the morning. Otis and I had classes later in the day, so it was odd Kam was here so early.

I had given him a key to my dorm a few weeks prior, so he could come around when he needed to get away from home, since he wasn't attending college. But that didn't mean barging in here at eight o'clock in the morning.

"Is there something you need?" I ask, standing to my feet to walk in his direction. He leans back in the chair, tilting his head to the side while showing his devilish grin.

"Two words. Frat. House."

I shake my head in my hands, dragging them down my face. He was seriously here to talk to me about frat houses? He couldn't even join one, unless he planned on attending the same college.

"No." My voice firm, turning on my heels to head back to bed.

"Think of it, Lip. We could all get a place together and have parties all the time. Then on top of it, think of all the ladies we'd meet."

My body turns back in his direction, hoping this is all a dream and that I'm still sleeping. "It can't work. You don't attend this college and it's probably too late to join anyways."

"That doesn't stop us from joining next year," he says, standing up to walk in my direction. "By next year we'll–I mean you and Otis will be seniors and I'll be a freshman if I apply to attend."

"Freshman can't join frats here. The rule for attending is you have to dorm your first year, there's no way around it."

Kam sighs, just enough to grab Otis' attention to wake him up. He rolls over in bed, facing our direction. "What are you doing here so damn early, Kam?"

A tiny laugh passes through Kam, swinging the dorm key in his hand. "Frat houses–"

"No," I interrupt, rolling my eyes.

"Why not?" questions Otis, pulling himself out of bed. "It sounds like fun and think of all the girls we could meet–"

Kam and Otis nod to each other, smiling at the thought that could never be a reality. I wasn't opposed to joining a frat, but it just couldn't be done in the way Kam was picturing it to take place. There was no way he could join a frat, first off he wasn't attending the school. And second, he would be a freshman at a campus that had set rules for their first years.

"No," I firmly input again, taking a seat on the edge of my bed. The two look at me, pleading their eyes like puppies to try and change my mind. But it's not going to work. "We can tour–*tour* frat houses to get an idea. But we can't join them."

"Then what is the point in touring if we're not going to join?" questioned Otis, rolling his eyes to glance over to Kam.

What was the point? To simply please Kam to get him off of his sudden fixation and to get his mind away from all the stressful things he may have built up in it.

"You know–" I hesitate, trying to think of the right words to say. "For the idea of the college experience. To see what a frat is really all about."

"He's bluffing," sighs Kam, rolling his eyes. "He could care less about it, he's just doing it to please us."

"Is that true?" Otis asks, turning his attention onto me.

I sigh, looking toward them. "Everyone is so caught up in their own things–Otis you're rarely here other than in the mornings and evenings because of your classes, followed by basketball practice afterwards. Then Kam, you're only ever here on the weekends. As for me, my social life consists of attending classes and sitting behind these four walls. I just think it's time for a change for us all to get out and do something fun. Even if that means not joining a frat, at least we're checking one out together to see what the future could maybe hold. And I said *maybe*."

Every word I spoke was nothing but the truth. Otis was so caught up in his basketball career outside of classes, that he rarely had time to get his own homework done. Kam tended to show up Thursday through Sunday to crash at our dorm, then other than that we never heard from him.

And my life wasn't anything I had hoped it would become. I wished everyday that my life would be like Otis' to have the college basketball career he had, to make it onto the big leagues. But I never could. I wished I could have a positive relationship with someone, but every time I tried, it only seemed to fail.

One failure only tended to lead to another. A grave I could never dig myself out of to have the life I dreamed it would have become.

If that one thing was never on my mind. I could've had it all. If it wasn't for *her*.

She ruined my life in all the ways imaginable and I'll never forgive her. Never forgive the thought of her ruining all the things I could've had. She made my life a living hell, each and every time she took another step closer.

One of the many reasons I ran when I had the chance. The only reason I failed to show up on the last day of high school, which I don't regret. The sight of seeing her would become a burning sensation in the back of my mind that could never burn out.

The memory of her is so vivid. Her hair burned in its red shade. She was like a fire that could hurt and that I could be burned by. Burned in all the ways I wanted to never forget all the pain she caused me.

I will never forget her. I will never forgive her.

Kam glanced in my direction, realizing my sudden attention had changed to be lost in a mindless thought. He coughs, grabbing my attention to allow it to shift away from my thoughts before he continues on with his rant.

"If you're sure about it, I'll check into tours to see what is available," he says, approaching the door.

I turn toward Otis, nodding before letting out a soft sigh. "Just let us know and we'll make something work."

Kam nods, opening the door to leave. He locks the door from the outside, hearing the turning of his key.

I let out another sigh, sinking down onto the mattress to press my hands against my head, running them through my hair.

"Are you alright, Lip?" Otis softly asks, filled with concern. He stands over me, glancing in my direction.

With all of my heart, I wanted to say I was okay–but I truly wasn't. The past two years haven't been what I had dreamed and I was afraid of where my life may end up if I continued on the road I was on, lost in a thought of all the what ifs.

"Don't you have to get ready for early morning practice?" I ask, turning my attention to stare out the window.

"I asked you if you were alright–clearly something is up if you change the subject." He takes a seat next to me, placing his hand on my shoulder. I turn to face him, attempting to hold a smile on my face. "You were once a captain who was always there for me, asking how I was doing and if I ever needed anything. Now that it's over, I need you to not bottle your feelings up and tell me how you feel. You want to be a therapist to help other people, when you can't even help yourself to explain your feelings."

The silence fills the room for a second, allowing myself time to think of a reply. "No–no, I'm not okay."

Concern fills Otis' face, not expecting such a negative answer in reply. He stands, walking toward his bag. He grabs out a basketball, tossing it in my direction. I grab it with quick reflexes.

"Pass the ball. Just like the warm-ups we used to do in elementary school when we were upset. You hold the ball, you say what's on your mind and how you're feeling about the situation," he says with confidence.

My fingers tap on the ball, sitting on my lap. I take another minute to think. "It should've been me–"

The ball tosses in his direction. "What should've been?"

He quickly throws the ball back, the anger flowing throughout both of our veins. "The scholarship. It should've been mine."

"And it wasn't–" He throws the ball harder with each throw. "Things happen for a reason."

"So Brielle happened for a reason?" The ball slams into his hands. "So you're saying the high school drama with her happened for a reason?"

Otis stands there, clenching the ball in between his hands. He lets out a sigh, throwing the ball back. "No."

"Then don't say things happen for a reason!" The ball lands in my hands, clenching it hard before tossing it onto the ground, knowing if we kept using it, it would end up hurting one of us. I rise to my feet, standing right in front of him. "I should've gotten the scholarship. I shouldn't have been involved with Brielle, and whoever caused that high school drama should've had an end put to them–"

Otis pushes my chest back with his hands, laughing with an eye roll. "Then I'm sorry. Sorry I didn't put an end to it sooner, Lip!"

I tremble on my feet, shaking my head in disbelief as his words couldn't be true. He was just saying it to rile me up. There was no way he could've caused the drama back in high school. No way possible, it wasn't him.

"Don't say that–" my voice cuts. The emotion racing through my veins, unsure of what to feel, knowing my best friend could've caused my downfall. "You didn't do it–"

"I did–" he hesitates. "But I didn't start it, nor did I end it. I just took a few photos and–"

"And I've heard enough."

Otis had tears in his eyes, which made me realize he didn't cause the drama entirely. He probably knew who did if he had taken the photos back then like he had said. But was it really worth my time of figuring out or even wanting to care?

It had been two years. Why should I still care?

I wrap my arms around Otis, pulling him in for a hug. "I don't want to know. It's better that way. You're a great friend and I don't want to lose you."

He smiles, holding my body tightly in the hug before pulling back to get ready for the day.

I wanted to know who caused the drama. But part of me wanted to let the past go to hope it would put my mind at ease for the future I could have. I had to think ahead, instead of looking back.

My body sank back onto the bed, while Otis got ready for his practice. I grab my phone off of the dresser to glance at it to notice there was a group text from Kam with random dates and times to check out frat houses.

I still couldn't believe he was so persistent on this topic, even though we didn't have a chance at joining one with him around.

Chapter Twenty

Brielle

Who knew all I needed was a girl's night to get my mind off of things.

The lights flashing in a vibrant shade throughout the club as Halle made her way back over to us from the bar with drinks in her hand. She sets them down on the hightop for us to grab.

I glanced over in Stella's direction, standing there with her brown curly hair pulled back as she wore a black sequin blouse with jean shorts. She didn't want to drink much tonight.

But Halle and I were all for the party, hoping it would put my mind at ease to wash away the thoughts of you know who.

"I'm still on for the idea of you leaving the letter in his gas tank!" shouted Halle over the loud music.

I roll my eyes, taking a sip of my drink. "Not one of your brightest ideas, Hal. I still haven't come up with anything to say."

"There's still time to think on it," Stella adds, pressing her elbows on the hightop. "It's not like you have a set date that you have to give it to him."

Halle and I nod, looking around the club to see there were people wall-to-wall. It wasn't an easy place to get around, as it seemed to be popular amongst the college population.

I glanced back toward Halle, who wore a red crop with ripped jeans. Her dirty blonde hair with red highlights was straightened tonight, brushed over her shoulders. "How about another round of drinks, on me this time?"

"I'm good for now. Thanks–" she shouts, leaning over the hightop.

But before she could finish her words, the DJ began to speak, lowering the music. "Let's get the karaoke party going, starting with the first group on the list. The Harrison Hot Ones!" Everyone looks around the club, as our attention meets Stella's wide grin. "Please welcome Brielle, Halle, and Stella to the stage!"

The club begins to clap, acting as if this is a normal routine for them. Stella's smirk never leaves her lips, walking in front of us to approach the stage.

"Stella you did not!" the two of us shout toward her.

"What? You can never go wrong with some *Lady Gaga* karaoke," she laughs, grabbing a microphone from the DJ. Halle and I grab one too, taking our places, hoping we don't mess up any of the lyrics. "You'll do fine, it's just *Paparazzi*."

The music begins to play, watching a screen of lyrics appear before us. Nerves fill throughout my chest, knowing I'll laugh this off when it's all over. But I'll have to find a good payback to get Stella next time.

I could definitely say my mind did go blank for once in my lifetime, standing up there with my girl's making a complete fool of myself as I tried to sing in the right key in front of the huge crowd.

But it was always impossible to match *Lady Gaga's* perfect tune.

The three of us walk the street, making our way back to my dorm on the outskirt of town. After I graduated high school, I didn't move far as I was attending a University in downtown Harrisburg. It was about a thirty minute drive from Harrison for the girls to travel here.

I open the door to my dorm, flipping on the lights to be met with silence. There wasn't much to see, being I shared a dorm with myself after my roommate decided to drop out during her first week of the semester.

Halle walks up to my desk, noticing my notebook flipped open to a blank page. The page I was planning on writing my note to Lip on. She picks it up, along with a pen to begin brainstorming some ideas and topics to cover in the letter.

"You want to tell him how you feel and how you felt with him, right?" I nod, watching her write it down. "Give me some other topics. This letter isn't going to write itself."

Stella takes a seat on the empty spare bed. "That writing this letter will give you closure and that you never meant to hurt him if you had in some way."

I stare at them, shaking my head. I take a seat at my desk, grabbing the paper out of Halle's hand. "I think I just need to write this by myself. Alone."

"We know how you feel and we hate seeing you this way. We want you to have closure with him if that's what is truly best in this situation," says Halle, walking toward Stella.

Stella nods in agreement. "You need to get your feelings out in the best way possible."

"I know," I sigh softly, sinking down into the chair to stare at the ceiling.

It was hard trying to find closure from something I never realized I needed until now. I never realized how badly it would hurt losing him, when we weren't even in a relationship to begin with. But yet from the very beginning I was warned and didn't listen.

Maybe Kylie was right, it would hurt more to let go of him, than if I continued to hold onto him in my mind.

I sighed again, lifting my body up to press my hands onto the desk. I force myself to grab a pen to allow the thoughts to spill onto the paper.

Halle and Stella watch over my shoulder as the words trail onto the paper. The thoughts and the things I always wanted to say came out of me with no control.

I couldn't stop now. But yet I did.

The pen came to a halt, clicking it closed to set down onto the desk. I glanced back toward the girls, faking a smile. "I think I'm just going to call it a night–"

They look at one another then lock eyes with me. Confusion fills their faces, letting it go as they approach the door. The two of them say their goodbyes, opening and closing the door to leave me alone in silence.

Alone at last.

I pull the letter up to my face, allowing the tears to fall. I read over the words once, not having the feeling of satisfaction fill my body to know this wasn't exactly what I wanted to say. It just wasn't right. Just not yet.

My hands fall onto the desk, crumbling up the letter with all of my bolted up anger to toss it into the trashcan on the other side of the room.

There was something about him I just didn't want to face yet. Something that was buried deep down inside of me that hasn't had the chance to be unleashed. There was still a part of me that came to be when it was only him and I.

Something I still hadn't discovered.

Chapter Twenty-One

Kam

*L*ip's stare is mindless, lost in the thought of the many frat houses we had spent the entire afternoon visiting. He wanted to deny his feelings that he felt this was meant for him. Meant for *us* as friends. But instead he chose to speak so negatively to continue to tell, even wanting to convince us that it just wasn't the right time.

"Maybe next year will be our year," Lip sighs, walking the path back to campus. "We've seen the houses, and I just don't think that we seem to be the right fit for them."

Otis rolls his eyes, kicking the autumn leaves out from between his feet. "That's your own opinion, and who says you can stop us from joining if we wanted to. Kam couldn't even join–but who says that I wouldn't want to join now if I had the chance?"

I glance over to face them, listening to the tone of their voices as they speak. It appeared their tension had been off for the past couple of days, ever since I brought the idea of frats up to them. Otis seemed to be on my side, while Lip thought the total opposite.

"You wouldn't," Lip snaps back harshly, glaring Otis up and down. "You're so caught up in your new lifestyle, with a dream that you never wanted. If you so badly want to join a frat, then just do it and see if I care–"

"You can't continuously keep being a controlling captain over us. You lost that role years ago, and it appears you haven't lost that high school ego of yours!"

Lip rolls his eyes, scoffing under his breath to stop in his tracks to stand face-to-face with Otis. "You know what, if you care so much about how I'm acting. How about you take a look in the mirror at yourself to see how much you've changed."

Otis pushes Lip's chest back, shaking his head in disbelief. "Watch that mouth of yours, Devonshire."

A sigh lets out of Lip's chest without a reply. I could say something to stop this. But why would I when the fire was only beginning to burn. One that could entirely be at my control if I so-what pleased to have it be.

"I'm done with this. Done with this argument," laughed Lip, taking a step back from Otis.

He glanced over in my direction, then back to Otis. "I'll meet you back at the dorms tonight."

Lip stormed off, leaving the two of us behind. Clueless of what was going through Otis' little head. One I learned to mend my way into so easily.

"What's his problem?" I finally speak, turning to Otis.

"I'm the problem–" he sighs, taking a seat on a bench off of the pathway. I drop down next to him, watching over his expressions. Studying him in every bit of detail. "The day you came over to mention frat houses, he and I got into a fight after you left."

"About what?" I curiously pry.

"He's jealous I got the scholarship and he didn't. I never knew he felt that way until now, and if I had known sooner, I wouldn't have accepted it. I wouldn't have taken it realizing how much that dream meant to him."

Lip was jealous–exactly what I wanted. The one thing that could ruin a friendship. *Jealousy.*

"Then what happened?"

Otis sighs, glancing over in my direction. "I told him–"

"Told him what?" I hesitate.

"He questioned if things happen for a reason, leading into what happened between him and Brielle, questioning if that was all for a reason. I told him no, so that lit his fuse to go off about her and then I told him...that I took the photos."

"That *you* took the photos," I repeat, in a tone that makes him believe it.

"I didn't say anything about you–and I wouldn't have. I promise. But he still didn't want to believe me that I caused it all. He knows someone else is behind it and I'm not sure if he cares that much to figure it out almost two years later."

I nodded to his words and I wasn't sure if I could believe him that he hadn't told Lip that I was behind this drama he longed to face. "You really didn't tell him?"

"I never would. I promise. I wouldn't do that to you, Kam, unless you asked me to tell him," Otis says, placing his hand on my shoulder.

He was truly a great friend. Just one I could never care about at the end of the day. Otis had a heart for those around him, while I had a broken one, that felt like an endless black hole that could never be fixed to care about anyone else but myself.

"But what if he asks again?" I hesitate, pulling back from him to stand on my feet. "What if Lip learns to question it and it eventually leads back to me?"

"It won't," he assured me, holding the confidence in his voice. "Lip and I have a lot to figure out, and it will all take time."

A slight smile tugs at my lips, as Otis stands up to begin walking the path again. I follow next to him, maintaining our conversation. "I know you had mentioned to Lip that if you had the chance to join a frat, would you actually?"

Otis nods, not holding back the thoughts he held in his mind. "I would–and it's something I had actually been considering long before you mentioned it. A few guys on my team mentioned it over the summer and asked me to join them. But I was so worked up and afraid of how Lip would take it, knowing he couldn't tag along with me since he wasn't on the team. So I told the team no, that I was dorming with someone already and I never mentioned the frat to Lip."

Even Otis had secrets that I didn't know, ones that were slipping out the more we talked. Ones that could tear his friendship apart with Lip, piece-by-piece at my control.

"Had you ever considered joining one with Lip? One without me being involved?" I question, hoping to get a truthful answer out of him. "You can tell me, it won't hurt my feelings."

Otis shakes his head in disagreement. "Lip never mentioned it, so I never did either. I know how Lip has always felt about you, that he never tends to want to leave you out of anything as much as I never seemed to understand it. He is a caring person who wants to care about others before himself, at least that's how he used to be before the jealousy got to his ego."

"Lip gave me a chance when nobody else did–" I stutter, glancing over in his direction. Otis has a puzzled look on his face. "When I first met Lip, he made me feel understood for once. He took the time to listen and care when nobody else wanted to."

"And after that you just tagged along?" Otis questions, still trying to understand me as he never saw the whole picture. "You just showed up one day, came to every practice and game and then started tagging along to the team dinner. But I never understood why."

"Because Lip gave me a chance. He allowed me to be seen–" I hesitate, feeling the emotion slip out of me in a way I didn't want to allow it to. "He wanted me to have friends. *A family–*"

"But you had a family that you could go home to, Kam–right?" he questions, stopping in his tracks to become filled with concern. "You didn't need to build one–unless you..."

"Didn't have one that cared," I finished for him, hearing the break in my voice. "My parents didn't care...they *still* don't care. That's why I come here on the weekends, to get away from them when I have the chance. I've never told anyone this other than Lip and my biological father, and now you."

Otis tilts his head, confused. "Your biological father? So you're telling me you have more parents in the picture?"

I nod slightly, turning my attention away from him. "My parents are actually my adoptive ones, who took me in to foster when I was younger. My real parents, my mother died when I was young and my father–Coach Becker, who you know really well, just let me go into the system."

"Coach Becker was your dad?" Otis is stunned more than anything, learning more about the person I am, other than the person he believed me to be. "How am I now just learning all this?"

"Lip doesn't even know Becker is my father, and I would like it to stay that way." Otis nods. "He is the reason you got the scholarship–because I told him to give it to you over Lip–"

"What? *No–*" Otis softly questions out loud to himself. "I earned that scholarship...didn't I, Kam?"

I shake my head in disagreement, feeling the adrenaline rushing through my veins to cause chaos with just the few words I could say. "I asked Becker if he could give it to you over Lip. You deserved it more than him and just because he was the captain, didn't mean he earned it. You were the one who made the points, not him."

"But I just don't understand. Kam why would you?"

Why would I? That's a funny thing to ask from a person like me. Truly why would I when it came to getting the one thing I wanted. Destroying the loyal trust shared between friends, to make them stronger and unbearable.

Destined for what fate lies ahead for them. No matter what it took.

"I did it for you, Otis. You would've never had a chance at the big leagues with him standing in your way. They were watching him as the captain in charge of the team. Not you. It took a lot of convincing to make Becker agree. But it meant having to take away Lip's chance for you to finally have a spot to shine."

Otis stands there stunned, glaring toward me unsure of what to say. Part of him looked mad, learning that he didn't want this position after learning how much it meant to Lip, to know he took it away

174

from his best friend. But the other part of him looked thankful to know I would do such a thing for him, despite the actions it took.

"Thank you–" he softly says, nodding once as he lets out a sigh of relief.

Thank you? That's all he had to say after learning how miserable I was making his life from this point forward, and somewhat he was thankful for that? Otis truly didn't make sense sometimes.

"Thank you," he repeats, so I could hear how sincere his tone was. "You really didn't have to do that." I nod, allowing him to continue on. "We all have our secrets, and I appreciate you sharing yours with me. So I will hold onto them, to not tell Lip as long as you can promise me that you won't tell him mine about the frat houses."

I nod lightly at his words, realizing he was on my side of the situation to hold back from telling Lip anything that he had learned tonight. To know that when the truth did eventually come out, it hurt a lot more than anything if they were being brutally honest with each other to begin with in the very first place.

Chapter Twenty-Two

Lipton

I could dream of her dying and I still wouldn't be able to get over her.

The thoughts trailing through my mind, entering into the dorm room alone to get some space away from my friends after our fight.

It had been a few hours since then and it took me that time to clear my mind. It allowed many of the older thoughts to creep back in, in the ways I hadn't wanted.

The thoughts of the one I wanted to escape. Run from if I ever had the chance. The thoughts of the girl I could've called mine if I took the chance when it was given. But instead, I allowed the thoughts of her to become a burden in the back of my mind of possibly letting her go too soon.

I wanted to run. I wanted to escape. I wanted to forget.

But I could never let the thoughts of Brielle go as much as I didn't want to admit it.

She caused me pain. She hurt what I could've had. She took it all away without a care in the world, not to realize how much my life depended on it.

A string I was still holding onto, afraid to let go. Uncertain of what the future would end up holding if I didn't continue to look back at all the what ifs.

Brielle was the one thing burning, that not even water could bear to put out with how much she's hurt me with each step she takes closer, it only makes me want to take two steps back. Knowing I would fall head over heels for her in a heartbeat if I had the chance.

But I couldn't.

Couldn't hold onto her, to know that the reason I'm in this dreaded situation is all because of her. She played the game to cause me pain. Without a care of who she hurt along the way, all that mattered to her was if she won the prize at the end.

Never to realize that we both lost it. To lose each other without hoping to look back.

I glance out my dorm room window, lost in the thought of Brielle, wondering where my life may have ended up if I gave her a chance. If we never fell into each other's pathways with the drama that was caused.

All leading back to my one thought. Who did it, and why did they?

The sound of keys rattling filled the void, hearing the sound of the door opening then shutting. The keys set down on the desk without a voice to follow. I turn over my shoulder, expecting to find my roommate. But instead, there stands Kam with his devilish smirk.

"You're not Otis–" I whisper under my breath, taking a step closer to him.

Kam shakes his head, plopping himself down in the desk chair. He clicks his tongue with a tiny laugh to follow. "You say that like it's a bad thing."

"It isn't–" I hesitate. "I just didn't expect you to show up here after what happened between Otis and I. We just don't want to put you in the middle of our problems."

He leans his elbow on the desk, placing his hand on his chin as he tilts his head to the side. He stares over at my presence. "There's something bothering you, isn't there?"

I take a seat across from him at the other desk on Otis' side of the room, shaking my head in agreement. "Do you think this is all supposed to work out?" A confused look crosses Kam's face. "With Otis getting the scholarship and my life not being what I dreamed it would have become at this point in time."

"I can't believe you're still dwelling on this, Lip," Kam laughs, pulling himself up to walk over toward the window. "Otis got the scholarship and you didn't. So stop acting jealous and get over it–"

I turn in his direction, shrugging my shoulders at his words. "But–"

"But you didn't get it, Devonshire. Life simply isn't fair," he interrupts with another laugh to follow. "So you need to focus on your future, instead of dwelling on the past you could've had."

"If I'm dwelling on it so much, then why do I still think about her?"

"Kylie?"

I shake my head, sighing as the sound of her name flows out of my mouth, like I've said it a hundred times. "Brielle–I can't stop thinking about what we could've had if I just gave her a chance."

"Nonsense," laughs Kam, walking back in my direction. "She made your life miserable–"

"She did, and now that I've recently learned as well, so did Otis. Along with someone else," I interrupt, watching his emotion quickly fade. "Someone didn't want her and I together for some odd reason. Someone caused the drama by posting those photos."

Kam rolls his eyes, scoffing to himself. "How did Otis possibly make your life miserable?"

"He took those photos. But he also mentioned it wasn't just him who was in on it. There was someone else."

"And he didn't mention who it was?" Kam questions, pressing his hand onto the desk to lean against it.

I shake my head, clueless of who could've caused this drama. I didn't want to believe that Otis could have been the only one behind this mess. There was someone else who he was working alongside. An accomplice who lurked in question.

"Otis didn't say a word. So I'm actually glad you came here, I was wondering if you knew anything about it," I say, inching closer to see the sweat begin to line his face. "Did Otis ever mention this to you while it was happening?"

A laugh lets out of Kam, glaring into my eyes with his smirk. "You expect me to know something about this. I could care less about getting myself mixed up in this drama. Otis can be a secretive guy when he wants to be, so maybe he was in on this alone."

Maybe he was. Maybe he wasn't. I really didn't know what to believe anymore.

But Otis was my best friend, which still made me believe he wouldn't have done something like this to have hid it for so long. He had no intention of ruining my life for absolutely no reason. Especially Brielle's life, when she did nothing wrong in this entire situation that she just happened to get wrapped into.

"What do you mean?"

"You don't think Otis has secrets that he doesn't tell you about?" Kam scoffs. "You don't know everything, rich boy. Money can't buy you the secrets your friends have, that you don't already know."

"What do you mean?" I repeat, raising an eyebrow with confusion.

"He did it. He took the photos. So let it go, and let him go." Kam firmly says, placing his hand on my shoulder. "It may be best if you want to move past this entire situation."

"What about Brielle? I did a lot of wrong things that I can't forget about. I treated her terribly and walked all over her when she was just trying to be nice. Then she got wrapped into this mess–"

"Just let the bitch go. She's nothing to no one now and not your problem to worry about, Lip. It's better that way," he interrupts, turning on his heel to walk toward the door.

I glance over in his direction, trying to comprehend his words in the way he thought the situation may be best in his eyes.

Kam was one of my best friends, other than Otis, who I couldn't let go. So there should be no reason he wanted me to pick sides to be able to move past everything that had happened. That was the fact of life, getting through those challenges you never wanted to face.

"Forget Brielle. Forget what Otis did. Forget what you faced in the past," Kam slowly says, opening the door. "It's time to move on, Devonshire. Start a new life to become who you want to be. Don't let her hold you back like she always has. Don't hold onto the bad luck charm."

The door shuts behind him, leaving me there to think in the silence.

He wanted me to be able to begin again. Be able to start a fresh new lifestyle in the way I wanted. But it wouldn't happen in the way Kam's eyes picture it, as I couldn't just let Otis go without an explanation.

I had to be able to look forward, instead of dwelling on the past of all the possible things I could've done differently. I had to have a fresh start, if that meant running from all the negativity when it came in sight in the rearview.

I had to forget her. I had to let her go. And I had to run like my heart was depending on the heartbreak of willing to let Brielle go, to know it was for the better. I had to escape her, once and for all.

Chapter Twenty-Three

Brielle

I could stare at romance books for hours, hoping one of them could one day be filled with a story like mine. But they never could if I continued to stand around here like a hopeless romantic without a story to tell.

I flip through the books on the shelves of the local bookstore downtown Harrisburg, hoping something catches my eye to get my mind onto something else.

For two weeks I had dwelled on the one thing I didn't want to face, truly didn't want to realize I had to face my emotions at some point in time. Those emotions that wanted to pour out of me like none other, but yet felt stuck in a way I couldn't explain.

The thought of Lip couldn't leave my mind. What I wanted to say to have my closure, and what needed to be done to do just that. The thoughts buzzed in a way I couldn't forget about them. Simply didn't want to forget if I had the chance.

I didn't want to let him go while I still had a chance to hold on.

In those two weeks I had dwelled, I tried to come up with a senseless plan of how I could get my emotions through to him. How I would be able to see him, or even how I would be able to get this letter into his hands.

The letter I hadn't quite written yet, only to wonder and want to come up with an idea to be in his presence again first before doing so. Afraid it might all just be a waste of time on my end if I took the time for the emotions that weren't spilling onto a piece of paper.

But one idea did come to mind, researching every local college's fall sports schedules to hope there might just be a game to support his school's team. The only problem was, I didn't know what one he attended.

There were at least three different options I could choose from, one of them being a football game that took place in a little over a week between my university and the Harris Hills campus. I felt in my heart, if any school he could have attended it would've been this one for sure.

I just had to listen to what my heart was telling me.

I had to trust myself.

I tug my notebook into my chest, turning the corner of the bookshelves to enter into the mystery section to begin looking through the books. Many ideas running through my mind of the right words to say, that I needed to place onto paper.

There were so many things I could say to him. So many things I could have done when the situation took place, to maybe make myself not regret this as much. There was always something in my mind that I couldn't ever seem to let go.

I had to have closure if I wanted to move past these regretful thoughts.

To have closure, you have to move past the pain. To face the pain, you have to forget it ever happened in the first place. And to love Lip, you have to let him go.

A thought begins to surface in my mind, one I was destined to have, pulling my notebook out from my chest to look at it, focusing only on that as I run into someone.

The body of a young girl stands there, around my age. She has short brown hair, styled in a bob cut as she wears a fashionable black outfit. I stare at her face, gathering my thoughts as I felt I had been in her presence before. That I had seen her somewhere.

"Are you alright?" the girl's voice quickly blurts out, reaching down to grab the book that had fallen from her hands. She glances in my direction with the same look, as if she knew me as well. "Brielle Johnston?"

I continue to stare at her, waiting for her to tell me her name before I make a lacking attempt at trying to remember it. I nod at the sound of my own name, allowing her to introduce herself.

She laughs, nodding, hearing my silence. "Sadie–Sadie Casper...I'm one of Stella's friends. We all went to high school together."

Her name still didn't ring a bell in my mind. But I felt like I should've remembered her if Stella had ever mentioned her in the past. But all of Stella's other friends had their own lives with her that I wasn't involved in.

"Yes...Sadie–I remember you!" my voice nervously laughs. "What are you doing here, in Harrisburg, so far away from home?"

"I work here actually. I moved here after graduation, got an apartment and wanted to start a new life to get away from Harrison. Smaller cities weren't my place to be."

I nod, moving past her to gaze over the bookshelf she stood next to. "Why did you want to get away from Harrison if you don't mind me asking?"

Sadie places the book in her hand into the right place on the shelf, sighing under her breath. "Harrison was full of drama, filled with small town gossip. I needed to get away from it and not be involved in it."

She was right about that. Harrison was nothing but drama that I knew first hand about. The drama I wanted to escape the second I became involved in it.

"Speaking of small town drama, weren't you involved in some way with that country club kid–what was his name again?" Sadie adds, placing her hand on her chin to think.

When I wanted to escape the thought of him. I never could.

"Lipton Devonshire," I laugh, rolling my eyes. "The self centered basketball captain and the man that held a spot in my heart for a reason I can't seem to understand."

"What ever happened with you and him?" she curiously asked.

I sigh, tugging my notebook tighter into my chest. "We both moved on. Went our separate ways to have a new life...but part of me still feels that I haven't truly moved on. I haven't had the closure I need to be able to get over him."

Sadie points at the notebook, as my eyes follow down to it. "What's the notebook for then? To write him a letter or something. To have the closure you want to have?"

Why was I continuing to go on to this random girl I had just met. She wasn't just anyone, she was one of Stella's friends. But still, why was I telling her this when she could probably care less about the drama I was mixed up into almost two years ago.

Why was Sadie so interested in trying to help me have closure when it was none of her business to begin with?

"It doesn't matter," my voice trails off, pulling back from the bookshelf to turn the opposite direction. "It's not like you actually care."

"In the little time we have talked, I can tell how much this has affected you, Brielle," she says, approaching my back. I turn over my shoulder to watch her concerned face. "He meant what words can't describe to you. Words that you can't put together."

"And that's why I came here—" I interrupt, pulling the notebook out to stare at it. "I just needed to find someone who could help me understand."

Sadie smiles softly. "Glad I was able to help you. I know we really didn't know each other much in school, but Stella talks nonstop about you when I see her. We'll have to get together sometime."

I nod, without a reply as I make my way out of the bookstore to approach my car with new ideas flowing through my mind. I open the car door, getting in to flip open my notebook as I click my pen to begin writing the words that would pour out of me with all my emotions to follow.

Dear Lipton,

I could go on to say a hundred words of all the things I could've said to you. But instead, here I am writing you a letter, unsure of when it will reach your hands, or if it even will. All the things I wish I could've said to you, I've held onto for years, for it all to come back to haunt me. The day I wished I had my chance at closure, it failed as I continue to look back at that one thing to believe I could've done differently to change that. To wonder if I was the reason you never wanted to be around, or if we just happened to be wrapped up into this mixed up situation for a reason that neither one of us will ever be able to figure out. But from that day I lacked having closure, I held onto each moment that we shared, as they felt like none other. You, Lip, taught me what true love could feel like in my heart and I want to thank you for that, as I never knew until I laid eyes on you that first day we met and talked all those years ago. From those sacred moments, it leads me back to wonder as well if I was the reason for your failed future. I know how much Kylie meant to you, and how much you held onto her like she was your good luck charm. But here I am, feeling as if I was the cause of the break up, that led to you not getting the things you wanted. I will hold onto that pain for the rest of my life, feeling that it was my fault, unless you could convince me otherwise as I don't expect an answer back from you. A failed response that I don't want to pry out of you, so I could have the simple closure I seek and want to have one day. Lip, I could go on for evermore, hoping I could get through to you. It always seemed your ego was set higher than the skies, that nobody could reach, nor tear down. For years I've held onto this regret, wondering and trying to find the right words to say. Possibly even needing reassurance that life would still move on without you. That life was worth living if I didn't think about you for the rest of my life if I had the chance too. The day I saw the sadness fill your face, I wanted to run after you to make sure things were alright. But I held back, afraid of making things worse as you realized you couldn't hold onto the game that was

191

your last shot at making a future you hoped to have. In the little we learned to know each other, it made me realize it hurt more losing you, than holding on to what I hoped I could've had. As you read this, again uncertain of where the fate lies ahead, I want to wish you the best, that you don't look back at all the mistakes you could've made. The mistakes that we got wrapped up in together. All of it, as each day passes by, only makes me want to say sorry a hundred times more than I already have in my mind. To want to wish you the best, to have the closure I seek to have, and the way fate was always meant to work out. A simple goodbye with all my love.

Signed, Brielle.

I clicked the pen shut, feeling the tears line my cheeks in a way I hadn't even realized I had begun crying. The open feeling in my heart, that everything had been lifted off of it for once in my life. The one feeling I lacked to have, now finally felt complete.

The sense of closure had braced my thoughts. The words I had always wanted to say had poured out of me like none other. The closure I lacked to have was now complete as I was whole and not broken by the thought of him.

The letter was written. The thoughts weren't a burden in the back of my mind anymore. The only problem was, getting this into his hands, if I ever had the chance to brace his presence just one last time.

Chapter Twenty-Four

Lipton

*T*he tension between everyone seemed to cool down over the course of the next couple of days. Otis and I talked out our differences, to come to a level of mutual understanding of what needed to be done for better communication between us.

As for Kam, who I felt was put in the middle of this situation, still appeared to be his normal self in his own little world that dealt with things in his own way. He never showed any signs of wanting to choose a side, or getting upset over anything that was happening.

He was still himself. The mystery he remained to everyone, but himself, that only I knew part of why he was this way. The stranger he lurked to be in everyone's minds, other than the ones he trusted.

I glance over in Otis' direction, as the two of us lifted weights in the college workout room. Sweat lined his pale face, and ran through his orange hair from occasionally brushing it back to keep it out of his eyes.

It was a bit of a workout. But we both knew it would be worth it in the end to keep our bodies in shape, even though I didn't need to work out as much as Otis had to, since I wasn't on the basketball team anymore.

"Are we still on for B-Dubs later?" Otis asks, glancing over in my direction, flipping his hair out of the way.

I nod, counting in my mind at the number lift I'm at, before letting out a breath to set down my weight. "Yep. We'll head back to the dorm after this to clean up and just meet Kam there."

"Is he still planning on coming?" Otis, lets out a breath while setting down his weight to lean on his elbows pressed against his knees. "I know he tends to bail at the last minute, that's only why I'm asking."

"I can shoot him a text to check."

Otis nods, as he stands to his feet, walking over to his gym bag on the other side of the room. I do the same, reaching down to grab my phone out of my bag that's placed at my feet.

I skim over my notifications, hearing the sound of Otis' feet approach me again. The sound of his fingers typing fills the silence.

"Coach texted me," Otis says.

"What, you got practice or something?" I question, glancing up toward him.

He shakes his head, stopping in front of me to text back a reply. "No. It's Becker. He says he's in the area and wanted to know if we wanted to meet."

Coach Becker, an old familiar face I missed seeing around everyday as stupid as that sounded. Hearing his voice, yelling at us to do our best when we were down over ten points on the board. To wonder, why was he texting Otis over texting me. His star team captain.

"See if he wants to meet us for lunch. I'm sure Kam won't mind," I say, opening my text conversation to inform Kam of the sudden change, wondering if he was still planning on joining us.

Otis nods, sending a reply to Coach Becker as I send mine to Kam.

Kam Larson

Me: 12:11 P.M.
Are you still planning on meeting us
for lunch at B-Dubs?
Coach Becker is joining. He was in town.
Hope that is alright.

Kam: 12:11 P.M.
Something came up.

I can't make it anymore.
Sorry.
Please save me some wings
if you don't mind.

Me: 12:12 P.M.
All good.
Let us know if you change your mind.
A seat is always open for you!

I glanced up in Otis' direction, rolling my eyes as I let out a light sigh that he could hear. "Kam backed out. No surprise there."

A laugh passes through him, sliding his phone into his pocket. "Let me guess, something came up?" I nod. "Typical Kam. Always a mystery to those who will never be able to understand him."

I reach down to grab my gym bag, throwing it over my shoulder as I laugh lightly at his message. "But he asked me to save him some wings."

"Of course he did," Otis laughs.

Coach Becker stares over our presence, amazed, but somewhat impressed by how much we've seemed to change in his eyes over just the course of two short years.

The man that had known us since we were freshman in high school, now learned to know us as juniors in college.

"What brings you to town, Coach?" Otis asks, reaching across the table to grab a wing. He dips it into a cup of ranch before taking a bite. "Harris Hills is a bit of a drive from Harrison."

Becker takes a sip of his beer, nodding at Otis' words. "I have family in the area and I figured I'd pay my star players a visit while I was here. That's if it's not a problem."

"We enjoy seeing you. It's been two years, too long," I laugh, grabbing a handful of wings to set on my plate. "We don't get much company nowadays."

Otis nods in agreement. "The only person we see anymore is Kam–" Coach Becker's attention shifts over at the sound of Kam's name being mentioned. Kam wasn't the brightest in his eyes. "He was going to join us for lunch, but backed out at the last minute."

"What a shame. It would've been nice to have seen him," Becker sighs, patting a napkin to his lips.

Coach Becker didn't talk to Kam much when we were in high school, which surprised me that he had reacted this way when it was mentioned about him not being in attendance. But neither did Kam talk much about him, other than the occasional eye roll whenever he tried to give Kam the best advice for the future.

"How is basketball going for you, Otis. Still working on coming up with those trick plays we practiced before graduation?" Becker adds, setting his napkin down onto his lap, reaching to grab a few more wings for his plate.

"It's still the off season, so there's not much game to play quite yet. But I go to the court every morning and evening to test my skills to make sure I'll have my all for when the pre-season starts," he replies with a slight head nod.

"What about you, Lip–how's life been treating you?" he asks, turning in my direction.

Like shit is all I can think to myself, without having the chance to find the right words. I fake a smile. "Could be better," I honestly admit. "Just wish I could have what Otis has."

Coach Becker smiles, holding confidence in his expression. "About that–" His phone begins to ring, interrupting his trail of thought. He pulls it out of his pocket, nodding at the caller-ID to quickly decline it. "There's a few things you boys should know."

Otis and I exchange the same look of confusion, wondering where this was going in Becker's mind.

"There's a football game, the homecoming game actually, at the high school next weekend that any of the sports alumni are invited to represent their class. I'd love to see you guys there, if you're able to make it. I know this is last minute," he adds, sliding his phone back into his pocket.

"We'd have to check our schedules. But I'm sure we could make it work," Otis says, nodding in my direction.

"Great. I'll let the sports director know, so that way we'll have enough food for everyone," he continues. "And another thing–" The sound of his phone begins to ring again, watching him roll his eyes as he glances at the same caller-ID. "I'll be right back. I have to take this real quick."

"Don't worry, we can just catch up another time," Otis quickly says, gesturing for Becker to leave. "We got the bill covered, go do what you need to do."

He smiles, standing to his feet to answer the phone to place to his ear, mouthing the words, thank you. He walks off, taking his sudden, somewhat urgent call.

I glanced over toward Otis, left with the wandering thought of what the other thing could possibly be that he was going to mention before the phone interrupted him.

"That was a nice visit," Otis joyfully says, taking a sip out of his water glass. "I wonder what else he wanted to mention. But whoever was calling, it seemed more important than a silly little conversation with two kids."

A silly little conversation–but clueless of what it could've been. To wonder in my mind, if that conversation was part of the reason Becker actually showed up here on a random afternoon.

There had to be a reason for his sudden appearance, and I didn't buy him wanting to see his star players, while he just happened to be in the area visiting family.

"It was nice," I sigh, reaching into my pocket to pull out my wallet. I placed a twenty on the table to cover my end of the bill and half of Beckers, while Otis covered his and the other half of it.

A smile fills Otis' lips as he leans back in his chair. I glanced over my shoulder to watch the crowd of people gathering in for the early dinner rush. Filled in my mind with the thoughts that couldn't leave them.

To be left with the one thing that remained a burden. Those things were always meant to happen for a reason in a way we could never seem to understand quite why.

Chapter Twenty-Five

Kam

The car door swings open, shutting behind as I glance over in the passenger seat to see the tall, firm body now filling the driver seat. A laugh trickles out of my throat, rolling my eyes once at his presence.

"You're late," I scoff, uncrossing my arms to stare at the man I hated to call my father.

Coach Becker clenches his hands onto his steering wheel, letting out a deep sigh that wasn't quite the sound of relief. But yet the sound of irritation. "Kam, you broke into my car and called me, not once, but twice, for what exactly?"

"Why are you in Harris Hills?"

A puzzled look fills his face, trying to hide the guilt that seeks to the surface within. "Answer my question first. Why did you break into my car? You realize with anyone else, that's a crime and I could press charges on you if I wanted–"

"But you wouldn't. I know you," I interrupt, leaning toward him. "I needed to talk to you. Is that a bad thing? A son, who wants to talk to his dear, loving and caring father?"

"You could've talked to me inside the restaurant. But instead, you're out here picking locks to get into places you don't belong!"

"I didn't want to see my *friends-*" I scoffed, pushing my finger into his chest. "They're nothing but a waste of my time."

"They care about you more than you'll ever know, and you're going to treat them like they're nothing?" he questions. "Kam, what do you really want?"

What did I want? Revenge-justification for what I could've had. A father figure who hadn't given me up at a young age, to walk away like I meant nothing to him. A life that I was deprived from having all those years ago.

A boy that was broken that was too tainted from ever being fixed.

"To know why you're here," I finally say, bringing my hand to my chin, staring at him with the question that fills my face. "What does Harris Hills have to offer you, that led you so far away from home?"

"This is why you broke into my car? To question why I'm here?" he laughs, rolling his eyes.

I nod, leaning back in my seat. "It's because you can't give up on Lip, isn't it? You're left with the dread of him in your mind not becoming the star player you dreamed he was capable of becoming one day."

His head turns to the side to gaze out the window toward the restaurant, falling into silence. He presses his elbow against the door to run his hand through the lacking bit of hair on top of his head.

"I got a job offer–" he sighs, shaking his head in my direction. "I was about to tell the boys before your calls interrupted our lunch. I was asked to be a fill-in coach for the upcoming pre-season at the university here, and if it worked out to be a good fit, they wanted to make it permanent."

I should've known. He could care less about his family, as the one who was sitting right in front of him, he had abandoned. Walking away as if it never meant anything to him.

"And let me guess, you want to give Lip another chance?" I interrupt. "Give me a break!"

He nods, agreeing that was exactly what he had planned to do with his role of becoming a new coach here at Harris Hills. But I wasn't going to allow it.

"What did the kid ever do to you, Kam?" he questions, showing a bit of concern. "All Lip has ever done for you is be there out of the kindness of his heart, and you treat him like this? I just don't get what he's done wrong."

I sigh under my breath, leaning up in my seat to get up close and personal to Becker. My finger presses against his chest to push him back in his seat. I glare into his eyes, feeling the fire burning within. "Don't give him the chance. He doesn't deserve it!"

"But why?" Becker pleads, wondering as he glares back into my eyes. "What did Lipton Devonshire ever do to you?"

What hadn't he done, I wonder to myself day-by-day. What didn't he have, that I could've wanted with my life. What did the rich boy of Harrison have that everyone wanted to have?

A wealthy family that was nothing but loving. A place to call home when times got bad, and a heart that was filled with care.

Everything that I was bound to not have. Everything I could never have.

He had the dream. He *lived* the dream.

Lipton was the man I envied of becoming more like, as I grew to know him. But I didn't want to grow to like the things he had that could simply buy me happiness when times would get tough. I wanted the things I craved to have, but never could reach within my grasp.

"Look at him and ask yourself, what didn't he do?" I scold. "Lip has the one life I dreamed I could've had. If I could die and do it all over again, I want what he has."

A laugh lets out of Becker. "You can make your life what you want it to be. There's nobody stopping you, but yourself."

I shot a glare in his direction. He had the nerve to say that, when he himself couldn't provide a helpful guide to get me onto my feet. He just expected me to fend for myself.

What a caring father he was–said no one ever.

"You really think that?" I laugh, inching closer to him. My hands make their way to the top of his shirt, grabbing onto the collar of it. "Take a second to care to think about my life–" A second ticks by without any reply from him. "Nothing. I have nothing worth holding onto. Nothing worth the life I could've had if it wasn't for you walking away. The life you had for only yourself–"

My hands grip onto his neck, pressing my fingers down to begin strangling him. I glare into his eyes, feeling a smirk begin to line my lips as I watch him fight for air and a chance at the life he had left to live.

"Kam–Kam, st–stop it!" he quietly breathes out, reaching his hands out to place onto my waist to push back. To fight for his life. But he became too weak as the air was slipping away by the second.

Any second now.

"Take a good look at me, your caring son, because I'll be the last thing you'll be seeing," I laugh, pressing my fingers harder into his neck. A cough of air lets out of him, pushing my grip looser. "You want me to stop? Just ask–oh wait, you can't!"

Any second now.

The tight grip held to his neck quickly became loose, allowing Becker to breathe freely as he pushed my body back into the passenger seat. He glares at me, wiping his sleeve against his mouth while trying to maintain a steady airflow.

No words follow his glare, but the subtle shake of his head to tell he was filled with anger. His son had just tried to kill him in broad daylight–I had tried to kill him.

The emotions begin to flow through me, trembling to find the door handle of his car to make my way out in a hurry. My breathing quickens and my feet race through the parking lot to get as far away as possible.

Chapter Twenty-Six

Brielle

"So what do you think?" I cheerfully asked, pulling the letter away from my face after reading it off to Stella and Halle as we sat in the parking lot of a bowling alley near Halle's campus. "It's not too much, is it?"

"You actually wrote that?" Stella's jaw falls in amazement.

Halle laughs lightly in amazement as well. "I can't believe she actually wrote something after she procrastinated for so long."

"So it's not too much?" I question them. They shake their heads to the side, both believing it was just the perfect amount. "Good. I was afraid I went a bit overboard with it. The emotions just seemed to pour out of me."

"But how do you plan on giving it to him exactly?" Stella asks. "That's the one thing we haven't come up with."

I shrug my shoulders, opening the center console of my car to place it in a safe and secure spot to come back to later. "We'll figure it out."

They both nod as we all exit out of the car to make our way inside the bowling alley. Halle heads up to the front desk to grab us a lane, while Stella and I make our way over to pick out some bowling balls for us.

"And he said I wasn't worth his time," a familiar voice says in the distance. *Too familiar.* I glanced over my shoulder, meeting the presence of Kylie Sanders who stood a few feet away, surrounded by a crowd of people. "Can you believe that?"

Her voice continues to laugh as it catches Stella's attention, who places her hand on my shoulder to make sure I'm alright. But my stare never leaves Kylie, left with the endless thought of how we happened to be here on the same night.

"Got us a lane. You got the bowling balls?" Halle's voice says, approaching behind us.

The sound of her voice catches Kylie's attention, glancing over with a smirk piercing through her lips. She pushes her drink into someone's hands, looking our bodies up and down as she makes her way over to us.

A man slowly approaches up behind her to follow her steps. Pale skin as he stood with messed up blonde hair and a brown sweater, with another sweater tied around his neck. The classic country club attire if I did say so myself.

"If it isn't Brielle The Homewrecker Johnston," the man laughs, pressing his hand on Kylie's shoulder.

I glare at him, watching his brown eyes roll at the sound of my name coming out of his mouth. But I stare at him as if I should've known him from somewhere.

"Rhett, let me handle this," Kylie laughs, nudging his hand off of her shoulder.

Exactly. I should've known.

Rhett Everhett. Graduated in the same class as us. Was the star quarterback of the football team, and possibly had even more wealth than Lip's family did, as his family owned a few car dealerships around town. So no wonder the two ended up together.

She was in it for money. Not what the relationship had to offer.

Kylie laughs, taking a few more steps in our direction. "What brings you girls to this side of town?"

"We were just leaving–come on, Bre," Stella demands, grabbing onto my arm to attempt to pull me away.

My feet stay flat, wanting to hear out what Kylie had to say. Maybe she wasn't the type of person she used to be anymore since Lip was out of the picture. What if Kylie had changed, being there wasn't a status to hold onto anymore like there was in high school.

"No. Let's hear her out," I whisper to Stella, glancing over to see Halle's concerned face as well. I turn back to Kylie, inching forward. "We're just bowling. You can join us if you'd like?"

A look fills Kylie's face, looking around at her friends to burst out into laughter. *There wasn't anything funny about what I had said.* "You want us to join you? As if we'd want to be seen with you!"

"Yeah, why would we want to hangout with the homewrecker? You kind of have a reputation we don't want to be following," Rhett inputs, holding Kylie's drink out for her to take.

I glanced back at Stella, feeling her hand clenching tighter onto my shoulder. She was furious. "If you say one more thing about Brielle, I'm going to–"

The two of us grab onto Stella to hold her back from lunging toward Kylie. This causes Kylie to let out another one of her wicked laughs.

"I'm just trying to play nice," Kylie says, taking a sip of her drink. "There's nothing wrong with a simple conversation."

"There's nothing simple about it, Sanders!" demands Halle, pulling Stella back to contain her in place.

"Enough," my voice pleads, toward both of them. I glance over to Kylie, believing I should've listened to Stella that it was better to walk away. "Let's go."

The three of us turn our backs to begin making our way over to our lane. But Kylie's end of the conversation wasn't quite over.

"You heard about the football game, right?" Kylie yells, just loud enough so we could hear. We stop in our tracks, turning to face her again, only feet away this time. "The homecoming game. It's this Friday. I'm supposed to let everyone know, being I was a part of the class council and I guess that goes for telling you too as well, Brielle."

I nod, taking the information in–taking in the perfect idea off of her words. The homecoming football game, the perfect chance at possibly getting to see Lip again. The chance to give him my letter.

It all made sense of how to move forward with my closure.

"We'll be there," I say, glancing over to the girls.

"We will?" they quietly questioned, that only I could hear.

I nod with a smile, allowing this new feeling to sink in of what could be the perfect plan for moving forward with my life.

The three of us start to walk to our lane, letting go of Stella's arms from being restrained to allow her to walk freely. This quickly backfires, as a smirk fills Stella's lips to turn on her heel to approach Kylie's group one last time.

What are you doing Stella?

Halle and I stand a far distance, watching her and unsure of what to do in this situation. That's until the sound of Stella's fist knocking into Kylie's lip fills the crowd with gasp and sudden yelling of a fight beginning.

Allowing chaos to unleash as the blood flows down from Kylie's now busted lip.

"Oh I've been waiting to do that!" Stella yells, turning back in our direction.

"Get them out of here. Now!" cries Kylie, pointing her finger toward the door.

A bartender makes their way over, grabbing onto each one of our arms to escort the three of us out of the bowling alley.

Remembering that night as none other as a smile lines my lips, sitting on the steps of the bowling alley. Filled with a sense of closure to know exactly what needed to be done to get this letter into Lip's hands, once and for all.

Chapter Twenty-Seven

Lipton

*T*he morning sunrise at the Devonshire country club estate could never get old staring at. Especially when you were all alone to take it in on this early Sunday morning.

I take my golf club, teeing the ball off into the distance without a care of keeping score of how many shots I had made during the morning.

It just felt nice to finally be home.

A sigh lets out of me, swinging my last hit as I bring my hand up to my forehead, watching the ball fade away. I clench the club in my other hand, making my way back over to the golf cart to grab another full bucket to continue on.

To my surprise there was nothing left, meaning I was going to have to call it early as much as I didn't want to. I set my clubs into the front seat of the cart, getting in to start up the ignition. I make my way across the course heading back to the cart storage dock.

I pull my cart in, quickly getting out to place my golf clubs with the rest of them and turning off the ignition to hang the key up on the wall with the other cart keys.

"Looks like someone's back from college early," a soft voice laughs. I turn to face the cart reception desk to see Sennedy standing behind the counter, leaning over on her elbows with a smile on her face. "What brings you back, Lip?"

A smile finds its way to my lips, meeting her presence. "I missed it, and the fact my mid fall break happens to be at the same time as the high school's homecoming game. So I figured I'd check it out."

She nods, walking out from behind the counter to approach me. She stands a few feet shorter still holding that same smile as she leans up against the front of the counter. "My friends and I were thinking about going to the game. But we're still not really sure."

"You should go. It will be worth it," I insist, inching past her toward the door as she turns on her heels to watch me. "Kam, Otis and I are all going. So you should too."

"Yeah, it will be fun," she laughs to herself. "Plus I'll get to see so many people that I haven't seen in years."

I nod, pressing my hand on the door to begin to open it. I looked toward the clock to notice it's a little before seven in the morning, and that meant the rest of the staff wouldn't be here for at least another hour. That really made me wonder why Sennedy was here already.

"Why are you here so early anyways?" I ask, taking a step closer to her.

"My shift starts at seven. But I like getting here a few minutes early to make sure everything is in order. Most of the golfers don't show up until after eight anyways. You've been the only one so far."

Well at least she was early to make sure she was on time, and seemed to care about her job, unlike most of the staff we had here who tended to show up late.

"It seems I forgot what this place was like," I laugh, brushing my hand against the back of my neck. "College has taken up most of my time. I rarely have time to return home to make sure things are in line here."

"Your parents have it under control, Lip. You don't need to stress about the family business—at least not yet," she says, turning to walk back to the counter.

I stare at her, remembering in my mind the girl she used to be years ago. The girl who I had spent a summer with and treated it like none other. The one who once held my heart so dear and close to her to not allow it to be broken.

That was all before Kylie came along to change who I was as a person.

Changed the way I looked at things, and the way I treated people.

Kylie did change me. Not for the better. But for the worse.

I was finally beginning to heal without her around.

"Sen-" my voice calls out, grabbing her attention to look over her shoulder. A smile braces her lips. "You know since the golfers don't turn up until around eight, how about you and I grab a bite to eat?"

She slowly approaches, rubbing her hand along the side of her arm. "Are you sure? I don't want to get in trouble with your parents."

"I'm sure. You won't get in trouble. I promise."

Sennedy lightly nods, following my lead as we make our way over to the banquet hall. When we enter, we're met with the silence of the empty room and only the sound of our footsteps to follow as we make our way into the kitchen.

She leans against the countertop, watching as I grab the eggs, milk, and pancake mix to place on the counter next to her. Her eyes never stray from any of my quick movements, beginning to mix the eggs up in a bowl.

"Don't you have staff for that?" she curiously asks, grabbing the eggshells off of the counter to place into the trash next to her.

I glance up in her direction, smiling at her words. There was staff, but there was still time before they arrived. So I figured I'd take this opportunity to make her something myself out of the kindness of my heart, and not let her go hungry her whole shift.

"What, you're just surprised to see Lipton Devonshire hard at work?" I laugh, grabbing onto the mixing bowl to walk over to the fridge to mix in some cheese. "I am still a human after all. I work just like everyone else."

A blush rises on her cheeks, quickly turning her head the other direction to avoid it being seen. "It's just–I didn't think you'd do this...for me–after everything we've been through. You know?"

I set the bowl back down onto the counter, reaching up to grab a pan that hung as I turned on the burner to allow it to heat up. "Sen, there's nothing wrong that happened in the past that you have to live with regretting. We dated. We loved each other, and just happened to move on with our lives after that one summer we shared."

She glances back in my direction, placing her hand on top of mine as she stares into my eyes. "She really did change you–Kylie. I know you hate when people tend to bring her up. But she really got into your head to make you think differently."

My throat bobbed at the mention of her name, nodding and realizing how true it was as much as I hated admitting it. "I know."

I pull my hand back from hers, reaching over to grab the bowl to pour into the pan, beginning to make an omelet. I reach over to grab the pancake mix as I slowly read over the directions on the back of the box.

"You're better off without her anyways," Sennedy softly says as she grabs onto the mixing bowl to place it into the sink on the other side of the kitchen.

I sigh, turning over my shoulder to watch her. There was something about Sennedy that could understand me like nobody else could. There was something special about her.

*T*he smell of strawberry covered pancakes and a fresh home cooked country omelet filled the Devonshire banquet kitchen.

Sennedy smiles, taking each bite of her pancake as she sits on top of the counter, while I lean against it eating my omelet.

I glance up in her direction, smiling at the sight of her. "Still think I need staff for this?"

She shakes her head, trying to hold back a laugh that wants to break free at my comment. Her finger swipes across her whipped cream on top of her pancakes to push onto my nose. A smile grows on both of our faces.

"They should be here any minute, right?" she asks, pulling her finger back to place on her chin to think. "I could use a second course."

My eyes roll as I reach over to grab a napkin out of the drawer to clean off my face. "Nice try. Not going to happen."

She rolls her eyes as well, glancing down to finish the rest of her pancakes.

"We got so caught up earlier talking about my life. You failed to mention something about yours. Are you attending a university, or is it just not for you?" I add, taking a bite.

"I take online courses. That way it gives me more time to put in hours here before the winter season hits." She nods, taking a couple more bites. "I've thought about attending an on campus class, but not sure exactly what one to take."

"What university if you don't mind me asking?"

"The one up in Harris Hills. It would be quite the drive to commute, so I'd have to dorm. Then that involves finding a roommate, which I'm not really sure about."

"No way, that's the same one I go to," I laugh joyfully. "I could give you a tour of the campus if you'd be interested, but no pressure."

She nods, taking the last bite of her pancakes to push the plate out of the way. She stares at me for a second as I finish up my food. "Thank you, Lip. You really didn't have to do all this."

I smile toward her, reaching out to grab ahold of her plate and mine to walk them over to the sink. I slowly approached her, brushing her legs to the side so I could stand in between them. I glance up into her eyes with the feeling that I could get lost in them for days.

Sennedy gently eases her fingers along my face, brushing them up to my hair. She softly smiles, leaning forward to brush her lips over mine. The feeling of her breath softly prickled against my skin.

"I don't regret it–" I softly whisper, staring into her eyes that were only mere inches away. "Loving you when I had the chance–"

Her smile widens, brushing her fingers down my hair and onto the back of my neck.

The sound of the kitchen doors open. The morning staff had arrived, conveniently on time for once in their lives at the worst time possible.

I pull myself back from Sennedy, rubbing my hand over my lips, not with the feeling of regret. Instead I have the feeling of dishonor to portray myself this way at my own place of family ownership. A place I would soon, one day call my own.

I had to learn to be an adult and not a foolish teenager I still believed to be.

"I should get going. The golfers should be arriving shortly," Sennedy said, pulling herself off of the counter. I nod once as she makes her way over toward the kitchen doors. She places her hand on them, looking over her shoulder. "You still have my number, right?"

I slowly approach her as I reach into my pocket to grab my phone out. I check over the contacts to see it's not in there anymore. Which meant Kylie must have deleted it when she had access to my phone.

She grabs ahold of it to type in her number, sending herself a text before handing it back to make sure she still has mine. "There. So we can stay in touch."

I grab the phone with another nod to follow.

"So we can stay in touch," I repeat.

Sennedy nods slowly, opening the kitchen doors with a smile to follow as she makes her exit. I glance down at my phone screen to admire the text she sent to herself with the short words of just saying the most simplest thing.

Hey.

A smile pierces through my lips as I slide my phone back into my pocket with this new feeling beginning to run through my veins. A feeling I hadn't felt in awhile to realize what it truly meant.

The feeling of falling in love.

Chapter Twenty-Eight

Brielle

*R*eturning home was the last thing I imagined I'd be doing on a day like today.

The breeze blew with the wind, cold and bitter as the September fall season began to creep in. Driving around these parts I grew up to call home my whole life, to return back to a place that somewhat brought me dread just thinking about.

Welcome back to Harrison. The place that held all those faded memories, stuck in the back of your mind that you just wanted to try and forget to hopefully move past them all one day.

The day that was approaching sooner than later.

My car pulls into the parking lot of the town's shopping center, parking my car to get out and admire the surroundings that I hadn't been able to embrace in quite some time.

It truly did feel nice to be home, at least that's what part of me told myself, hoping to bring that part of myself the closure it needed to have.

I take in a steady breath, swinging my purse over my shoulder, while shutting my car door to make my way to the first shop. That was the thrift store that always tended to fit my style and a place where I could upcycle any old belongings to find a new use for them in some sort of way.

My body guides its way throughout the store, dragging my hand along to flip through the selection to look at every bit of detail it holds.

It was nice being back to where I felt like I belonged. Taking in the memories this place held in my heart as I let out a deep sigh.

"This one looks nice. Doesn't it?" a soft female voice speaks, an aisle over.

My feet come to a halt, pausing in my own tracks to glance around the thrift store. That voice–I knew it from somewhere. But I couldn't remember exactly where.

"You should totally try it on!" another voice speaks, in reply to the girl.

I glanced over my shoulder, catching a glimpse of her long dirty blonde hair and her joyful expression that lingered on her face.

Sennedy Marie. *What was she doing here?* Especially at the same time as me?

I quickly hunch over behind a clothing rack to hide myself from her. *Why was I hiding, she was my friend–right?* Peeking my face out an inch to continue overhearing her conversation with a girl that appeared to be our age.

You're such a coward, Brielle.

"Maybe it would be a good date outfit with you know who," Sennedy laughed.

You know who? Who was she talking about?

"You won't believe what happened the other day," she adds, hearing her footsteps make their way down the aisle. I slowly inch next to them to overhear, still without being seen. "I thought it was just going to be a simple Sunday until he showed up. I was working the morning shift and there he is, walking in like he owns the place–"

"He technically does, Sennedy," the other girl interrupts. "It's his family's country club after all, that he'll one day take ownership of."

*Country club–*were they talking about Lip?

"So after he walks in, he turns in his keys and clubs and then he offers to go have breakfast at the banquet hall. I thought out of anyone, his staff would make our meals. But the man himself made them, which shocked me," she says, rummaging through the clothing rack.

"You're telling me, Lipton Devonshire cooked you a meal?"

So they were talking about him–which meant he had to be home. At the same time as me?

"That's not all," laughs Sennedy, taking a couple more steps down the aisle. "The meal was great, and so was the kiss that was going to happen. Until his staff interrupted it from happening."

A kiss–they almost kissed? I didn't even realize they still had feelings for each other, after everything Sennedy had mentioned years ago about the summer fling they had. I just figured it was nothing to worry about.

"So you didn't even kiss him?"

There's no reply from Sennedy, so I take it as a side shake of her head to mean nothing else happened except him cooking her a meal.

"I wouldn't have minded the kiss," she softly admits. "But we were just mere inches away from it being real. I gave him my number and he offered to give me a tour of campus if I was interested. So I know there's more to us if I want to give it a chance to happen."

The other girl doesn't reply, as the two of them turn the corner to move into another aisle, two rows over to become out of my hearing distance. I rose to my feet, glancing around the store to make sure I wasn't being watched, or even caught by them.

I couldn't allow my cover to be blown, especially after obtaining this new information about Lip and his possible new relationship that Sennedy wanted to grow with him. But the thought of Lip gracing my mind made me want to wonder if she was right.

Was he really back in town, conveniently at the same time as me? Or was he just visiting for the weekend, as I didn't even have a clue of what university he was attending and how far away it was from here.

I slowly make my way back out to the car to get in. I pull out my phone, opening a text message conversation to alert Stella of the new information.

Stella Monroe

Me: 4:47 P.M.
*You're not going to believe
what I just found out.*

Stella: 4:48 P.M.
Do tell...don't keep a girl waiting!

Me: 4:48 P.M.
*I just overheard Sennedy at the thrift store.
She said Lip's back in town.*

Not sure if it's true or not.
It might just be gossip.

Stella: 4:48 P.M.
So what about your original plan
Ya'know to give him the letter?
You stalked every college campus,
hoping he'd be at one.
You can't tell me you're backing out now.

Me: 4:49 P.M.
No. Not exactly.
I'll still give him the letter.
I just have another plan.
A better one.

A smile grows on my lips with a new thought in mind. If everything Sennedy had said was true, that really meant Lip was home. And if he was home, that meant I had an even better chance of seeing him to be able to have my closure.

A chance to admit my feelings. A chance to fix what was broken. A chance to make everything better from what it once was.

I was finally going to be able to say goodbye and fix what should've been done a long time ago.

I was going to get Lip back.

Chapter Twenty-Nine

Kam

This. This was all for a stupid football game?

A smile crosses both Lip and Otis' faces sitting in our normal spots at Nick's as we enjoy a slice of pizza, just how old times used to be shared between us back in high school.

"I forgot how good this place was," laughs Otis with a mouthful of food.

I glared at them, leaning back with my arms crossed in a chair while the two sat directly in front of me.

As much as being home felt like a joy for them, it wasn't the same whatsoever for me. I dreaded having to come back here, being placed in this position as all I wanted to do was run and escape from it.

"Aren't you going to eat, Kam?" questioned Lip, pointing toward the few slices that were left on the tray. "You can take the rest home if you want."

"But–" Otis pleads as he attempts to grab another piece.

"I'm fine. Not hungry. I've actually lost my appetite," I say, looking down at the food to push in Otis' direction. He quickly grabs a slice to throw on his plate. "I might just head home. It's been a long day."

The two shoot each other looks, confused before they look back in my direction.

"Are you sure?" Lip asks.

I nod once, staring at him as he shrugs his shoulders to continue eating the slice of pizza in his hand.

"Why are we back here again?" I finally speak, leaning my elbow onto the table, pressing my hand to my chin.

"There's some sort of celebration going on for the class alumni at the homecoming game this Friday. That's according to Becker," Otis says.

It was already Wednesday. This week couldn't move by slow enough.

"It will be fun. Seeing our old classmates," adds Lip with a nod.

I roll my eyes, leaning back in my chair again while running my hand through my hair. "To see Brielle. That will be fun for you?"

A confused look passes over Lip's face, with a slight blush to follow. "No. I just said to see our old classmates. Plus she probably won't even be there. Sports games weren't really her thing."

God what did he see in this girl?

"Sure," I laugh, rolling my eyes at the thought of it. "Now what do you plan to do if she is there?" Lip shrugs once, clueless of a plan. "Run. Run from her."

"Why would I do that?" he laughs, mirroring my image to lean back in his chair. "Yeah she did make my life somewhat miserable in high school. But part of me misses that–"

"Run," I repeat, firm enough for him to understand. "That's it, she made your life miserable back then. So what makes you think she won't do the same now?"

"It was just a silly high school crush that became a joke. A cute one at that," inputs Otis, taking the last bite of his pizza slice. "Bipton was a thing. Trending trademark name."

The two of us shoot a glare in his direction, as he laughs it off to allow us to continue our conversation.

"She's going to try and talk to you, Lip. You have to tell her to leave you alone and stand your ground. She's toxic and will ruin your life more than she already has," I add, leaning forward to press my hands against the table to stand up.

Lip stares at me, taking in my words. Unsure if he will allow them to over take him, to control his mind in the ways I wanted them to.

He had to know that a flower as dull and soft as Brielle, wasn't always as sweet as they once may have seemed. Most times they were sharp, as it only took them time to grow their thorns to stab you in the back.

"She won't be there. There's no way," Lip speaks, confidence held in his voice. Maybe she wouldn't be. We just weren't sure. "And if she is, I'll run—like my life depends on it."

So he does listen, exactly how I wanted him too.

Good.

"I'm going to call it a night," I say, changing the subject to step out of the booth. A nod passes from both of them, standing to their feet to call it a night as well.

"We'll pick you up at four on Friday. Does that sound good?" questions Lip, approaching me.

"Why so early?" I ask, taking a step back to make my way over to the door.

"There's the homecoming parade before, so I figured we'd go to that. Plus it avoids all the traffic afterwards."

I shrug lightly to go along with anything he said. It's not like I had a choice, it was better being with them as I hated to admit than being stuck at home.

"Just text me, and we'll figure it out." They smile with a nod as I open the door, exiting out of the restaurant to make my way to my car to head home.

*H*ome is a place I lack to want to call my own. A bitter cold feeling fills my heart, entering through the doors of it.

"Someone's out late again," a woman's raspy toned smoker voice says to catch me off guard. Standing a few feet away in her pajamas stood my adoptive mother with her hands on her hips, holding a cigarette. She didn't look too happy about it. "You're over eighteen, it's time you found a place of your own."

I roll my eyes, passing through the living room to avoid speaking to her as the presence of my adoptive father approaches. "Your mother is speaking to you. It's time you showed her some respect."

A light sigh lets out of me. I turn around to face her with a fake smile lining my lips, scoffing at the sight of her. "What, the state income you've gotten over the years can't afford to support me anymore?"

"Watch your tone with me, young man," she demands, pointing her finger in my direction as she takes a step closer.

I slowly back up, nodding gently at her words while holding my hands up defensively. She didn't scare me, she intimidated me more than anything. "Fine. If it's the problem you make it out to be. I'll be out after the weekend."

"You better be," my adoptive father scolded. "Out by Sunday night at the latest. No excuses."

I nod to make my way down the hallway to my room, letting out another heavy sigh when I close the door behind me. I didn't have a plan of where to go, nor would I want to think of one.

This house wouldn't function without me. My parents were in one of their drunken moods they tended to get into late at night when I was gone. There was no way this would last long.

In the years I had lived here, it was always uncertain of what I could come home to, or wake up to in the morning. The house would always be a mess and I would have to be the one who took care of it all if

I wanted to continue calling it my home as much as I hated it.

As much as I despised it, it was still a roof over my head at the end of the day.

My body sinks down onto the bed to run my hands through my hair, taking in everything that was going on around me.

As badly as I wanted to escape. I still felt like I had no choice. No better option to help myself.

Yeah–there were people who would take me in out of the kindness of their hearts. But I didn't want to put myself in that position of being their responsibility over being their friend anymore, such as Lip.

Maybe even Becker might–if I hadn't pulled what I had at the restaurant last week. But at the same time, I was still his actual son and I knew deep down he wanted to care about me.

But I was an adult, not someone's child who needed to be looked after. Even though I still felt and acted like one for the most part.

I needed to grow up.

Another sigh lets out of me as I rise to my feet to pace around my bedroom. This house was filled with memories, many I hated looking back at to know I was wronged from having the good ones. To know my life could've been better if one thing had changed. If I hadn't been placed in this house–it all would've been different.

I would have been different.

The sound of footsteps approaches down the hallway, getting closer to my room by the second. My bedroom door swings open as my eyes dart to it, to see the firm figure of my adoptive father standing there with a glare in his eyes.

Within a second, it all changed. Instantly, what felt like my life was flashing before my very own eyes took a turn. His body made its way across the bedroom to slam my body forcefully into the wall, with no way to defend myself.

A twisted smile filled his lips, seeing the haze in his drunken expression. He holds both of my wrists above my head with one hand, as his foot pinned down on both of mine to allow them to not move. His other hand holds a broken beer bottle to my neck that left shattered glass around us.

"I've told you to watch that tone of yours," he scolds, smelling the alcohol on his breath. "Your mother is out there crying because of you. What do you have to say for yourself?"

I glare at him. There was nothing I wanted to say. But part of me wanted to say everything that had been on my chest, for years being placed in this position. "She's not *my* mother–and you're not even *my* father."

The bottle presses in harder, the glass cutting my skin to allow the blood to flow. A laugh lets out of him, pushing me harder against the wall. "We gave you a home when you had nothing–"

"Nothing, which I'm fine with if it means getting out of this hellhole. Getting away from you!" my voice raises. I attempt to push him back, but he's too strong and I'm too weak. Years of practice didn't make up for trying to get out of this. "There's someone that loves me out there–"

"Nobody can love a man like you. You're too broken. Too gone. For having someone who cares about you," his voice interrupts, firm in his tone. His last words come out slowly. "That's why your real family left. They didn't love you."

My heart beats through my chest, holding back the tears on my eyelids. I knew that wasn't true, but his voice seems to speak what would have sounded like the truth to myself years ago if I had heard it then.

I knew differently now what love could feel like. A feeling I had only felt a few times in my life to wonder if that was something I was meant to have. To believe in those times I felt it, it was for a reason I couldn't understand.

I could be loved, and I could love if I wanted to allow my heart the chance of doing so with someone.

"No. *No*...that's not true," my voice quivered with one last attempt to push his body off of mine. "No, that can't be–they did love me and they still do!"

The smirk remains on his face, hearing the sound of his beer bottle dropping onto the floor. He quickly backhands my face to push it the other direction. The stinging burns through my cheeks, slightly turning back to face him as his hand makes its way down to my neck to push against it with the rest of his force.

He was so strong and there was nothing I could do.

"Watch your tone!" he yells, dropping my hands down from above my head that now felt weak without any blood rushing to them. They rest at my sides, as his hand repeatedly begins to hit my face over and over again without a care that he was hurting me.

The abuse.

I couldn't face escaping it. Just couldn't bear the feeling any longer.

With every vein that ran through my body, it took the worth that was left to live right out of me.

Just please let it stop, I'd plead softly to myself, hoping it was all just a figment of my imagination.

Stop. Please. Stop.

With every beat of my heart, that pulsated with every breath taken. Every hit made–I couldn't be free.

I just wanted it to end. Wake up from this dream that was nothing but a nightmare.

His hand pulls back from my face, glaring into my eyes as he shakes his head, looking accomplished at what he had just done. My weakened expression stares back at him. The feeling in my hands slowly comes back.

"Watch my tone?" I laugh back at him. A smirk grows on my lips with the blood that runs down my face. My hands find their way to his chest as I spit in his face. "You watch your actions–"

The force of my hands pushed him back into my dresser, stumbling over his own feet as he tried to make it after me, moving my way around him quickly to race out of my bedroom. His voice is the only thing that follows me, making my way into the backyard.

I slowly backed up, trying to catch my own breath while also making sure he didn't decide to run after me to lash out the remainder of the anger he still had. I begin to run my hands through my hair, sinking to my knees on the wet cold ground.

The rain poured as the thunder rumbled beneath me. My emotion slipped from my eyelids, dropping the tears onto my warm cheeks from where I was hit. This was my life. The one I couldn't escape as badly as I tried. I would always end up back here.

A breath lets out of me, replaying the night back over in my mind, to think of how it started out so carefree, to take a turn to become so cruel in a blink of an eye. I didn't deserve this. Nobody did.

My hands press against the ground, grasping the dirt with the outstretch of my fingers. I cling onto it, taking it into my palms while falling down onto my elbows. My hands slowly open to look at it. Even the dullest things could be beautiful if they were given a second to be cherished, more than just being walked all over.

The dirt melts out of my hand from the rain, allowing my body to sit upright on my knees. I glanced around the backyard, watching my eyes mend their way to something new. An object that shined in the moonlight, wanting to be seen.

My body creeps across the dirt on my hands and knees to approach the object. To see in the better light, there sat a baseball bat that had been left behind from the summer prior. Most likely one of those days when I had nothing better to do, than clear my mind by hitting a few pitches into the yard.

I tightly grab onto the bat to tug it into my chest. An idea comes to mind, sweeping over the old ones. The darker ones. An idea that wasn't one of my brightest, rising to my feet to swing the bat in my hand.

Don't, a voice in my mind spoke, feeling my feet beginning to approach the house. *Don't do it, you'll regret this*, another one spoke. My feet came to a halt as my hand clenched the door handle to the back patio entrance.

Why was I doing this?

I throw the baseball bat over my shoulder, pulling my hand away from the door handle. I turn on balls of my feet to slowly approach the backyard again. A sigh lets out of me, swinging the baseball bat off of my shoulder and dropping it back onto the ground.

I was going to kill my parents–for what reason exactly. *Anger?* The justification I wanted to have, or even the revenge that was long overdue in my mind. The reason I could never bring myself to realize, that no matter what, I would never be happy.

If I wanted to kill them, what satisfaction would that bring me? Watching them bleed out and then getting a few seconds to laugh about it, just to spend the rest of my life in prison over a crime I never meant to commit. An act that was meant to be seeked out of the revenge that I craved to have one day to possibly bring myself some closure to have a brighter future.

No matter with any wrongdoing that was done, you could never fix what was already broken. A mistake you may have made, was meant to have happened for a reason. But with every action that was made, and with every person you have ever met. It was all meant to have come into your life for a reason you may never bring yourself to realize quite what for.

A reason you may want to escape. A regret you may want to forget. An action that rippled like dominoes that never seemed to come to an end.

To realize one thing, as bad as my past may have been, I was placed here today for a reason. Unsure exactly why, despite all the things I had done leading up to this point. There was a reason I was meant to return to Harrison as much as I didn't want to in my heart, my mind wanted to tell me otherwise.

Chapter Thirty

Brielle

*W*hen I stare at this letter, all I want to see is his eyes staring back at mine. To hope to have the sense of closure I lacked to feel. The part I *craved* to have. The part that ran through my veins to know the day had come, much sooner than I had hoped.

"I really don't think I should take it, Stella," my voice pleads, lifting up the center console of my car to stick the letter in there. Out of sight, out of mind. We stood in the high school parking lot, staring at each other, both filled with different options on this entire situation. "I don't want to lose it, if for some reason Lip isn't actually here. You know?"

Stella's glare is strong, rolling her eyes to reach in to grab the letter out of the console. "Take it. It's better to have it, than not have it at all if he is here."

I roll my eyes, while Stella opens my purse to stick the letter inside, making sure it was in a safe, secure location. The car doors shut to begin making our way up to the road to watch the parade.

"Sadie should be here," Stella adds. She pulls out her phone to text her to find her location. "She says she's down toward the beginning of where it starts."

I smile with a nod. When I first met Sadie last week, we hadn't been able to get the chance to talk again with our busy schedules. So I was looking forward to being able to get to know her more, or just having it be a way to take my mind off of you know who.

"I never thought this day would come," I admit, turning in her direction as the two of us walk along the roadside. We both wore the school's color of a dark burgundy to show support to the team. Stella glanced over, a confused look crossed her face. "I figured I'd be able to give him the letter at one of the college games I spent hours searching for. Definitely not coming back to our roots to be back at high school, replaying this whole misled love story over again."

"It would've been impossible for you to have found him at a college game. You didn't even know what one he was attending."

I blush slightly, turning my head the other direction. It wouldn't have been impossible as Stella put it, since she didn't know the whole truth to it. After thinking long and hard about it, I was able to do a little more research to figure out what college he was attending. That was Harris Hills, and it just happened to be the same college football game that was playing tomorrow, if all else failed for us tonight with getting the letter in his hands.

But that was another problem to deal with at a different time if it ever came down to be.

I turn back in Stella's direction as we approach closer to the beginning of the parade. "In my mind, I would've made it look easier than you make it seem to be. I know what type of car he drives, so I'd put that information together to be able to find him on campus."

Stella's voice turns into a soft laugh, throwing back her head. "Brielle, you're crazy."

Crazy, yeah–yeah I was. Crazy in love? You could say that also. But crazy psychotic, we don't know about that one yet.

"There you are!" a voice joyfully yells in our direction. A figure of someone runs into Stella's arms, latching onto her with a tight hug. "It's about time you showed up. The parade is about to start."

The figure pulls back to notice her joyful smile, to see Sadie standing there with her short brown hair brushed back behind her ears and as well wearing the same shade of burgundy to support the team.

"We would've been sooner if it wasn't for Brielle taking up so much time debating over her confession about a guy," laughs Stella, turning in my direction.

A curious look possesses Sadie, to wonder the story behind it. "A confession? To whom if you don't mind me asking?"

I reach down into my purse to grab the letter out. I hold it up in Sadie's direction for her to read his name on the outside of the envelope. "A confession to Lip. I needed to get my feelings out and the girls convinced me writing them down to give to him would be the best option. But we're not even sure he'll be here."

Sadie nods, grabbing onto the letter. I quickly tug it back in my direction, not allowing her to read it as I slide back into the secure spot in my purse.

"Just let her read it, Bre," Stella begs, tugging on the side of my purse. I place my hand over it to hold it shut. "Then she'll know the story behind it more. You let me read it, so why not one more?"

I glanced up in Sadie's direction, shaking my head once at the rejection of allowing her to read a letter I held so dear and close to my heart. The confession I had spent weeks trying to find the right words to say. That I wasn't going to allow it to be read off to everyone.

"It's fine. It's her letter anyway," Sadie says, not letting the smile fade off of her face.

Stella turns silent as she glances over in my direction with her puppy dog eyes to plead my point. But I wasn't going to budge, as my emotions weren't something I wanted to mess with sooner than I had to tonight.

The high school stadium crowd was roaring in the stands louder than any other game, as the three of us took our seats in one of the very few spots that was left.

"I rarely went to games in high school. But I don't ever remember them being this crowded or loud," I shout just loud enough for the girls to hear, over the sound of the band that was playing next to us, while pointing toward the rest of the stands.

Stella glances over in my direction, covering her ears from the noise. Her voice speaks in a loud tone as well. "Me either. But the game should start any minute now though, so the noise won't get any better."

A smile slightly crossed my face, turning in the direction of the field to see the scoreboard had a countdown of a little over three minutes left before the first quarter started.

Being back here didn't seem to bother me as much as I thought it would have. The feeling of coming back to my roots, to allow everything to resurface that I had pushed away in the back of my mind for so many years. It just didn't phase me to allow it to bother me in the way it should have.

But maybe it was the part of being around the ones I trusted the most, that it allowed the burden to not become loose in the way it would have years ago–around him.

The sound of joyful screams filled the stands even louder as the sound of the buzzer went off, marking the start of the first quarter as the players made their way onto the field. Everyone cheered for their team, or even favorite player, as us girls were just cheering to have a good time.

My eyes watch the field, to study each and every player, trying to remember if any of their jersey names or numbers looked familiar from when I roamed the halls here. But it seemed impossible as my eyes find their way down to the end of the field, noticing a tent behind the goal post that appeared to have students underneath it.

But why did this want to grab my attention?

I tilt my head to the side, studying each student from a distance as many appeared to be unable to read who they were in my mind to remember them from this slight detail.

My eyes trail over one in particular, feeling my heart drop, maybe even stopped at the sight of him. The sight of the one I knew every bit of detail about, to the color of his hair and the softness of his skin.

I reach into my pocket, grabbing out my phone to open my camera. I hold it up in his direction, zooming in the focus to get a better glance at what may be true in my eyes. To allow my delusions to not get the better of me tonight.

My stare is endless, tugging my phone back down in my lap and allowing my jaw to fall open in shock. My heart is beating in an unsteady rhythm, as my hands begin to shake. A smile twists its way onto my lips, laughing lightly under my breath out of pure and utter shock.

He was here.

Lip was here.

Chapter Thirty-One

Lipton

Run. Run from her, Kam's firm voice repeated in my mind every time I thought about returning here tonight. The night that I wanted to feel endless, pushing away all the feelings I may have felt over the years, being placed back at our old high school.

The thought of Brielle, wondering if she was here, lurking in the stands to be watching out over me like I was hers and she was mine.

I couldn't think like that. I didn't want her that way. I wanted to push her aside, as if she was nothing, and nobody to me. Allow the burden of her to fade into darkness, to never think of it again.

I had to let her go. Tonight if any night.

A sigh rolled out of my chest, turning to face Otis as he talked with Coach Becker underneath a tent while the game played out on the field.

I glance around quickly, listening to bits and pieces of their conversation, beginning to wonder where Kam had wandered off to. It wasn't like him to go off on his own, but I knew he didn't want to come to the game tonight either.

So maybe it was best for him to take a minute to breathe and walk away from the situation he could have felt an outsider in, being Coach Becker was here and that didn't seem to be his favorite person to be around lately.

"They sure are losing, aren't they," laughed Coach Becker, shaking his head.

"It wouldn't be a homecoming game if they weren't," adds Otis with a nod of agreement.

I turn to face their direction, shaking my head slightly to change the topic of the conversation that was being had between them. "Has anyone seen Kam?"

"I think he headed over to the concessions," says Otis, looking over my shoulder, attempting to find Kam somewhere in the distance.

My attention moves over my shoulder to look over toward the scoreboard. They were down *14-28*, with a few minutes left in the game. There was no chance of them coming back to win this.

"I'm probably going to head out, if it's not a problem with you boys," says Coach Becker, patting his hand on both of our shoulders. "It was nice seeing you again, and tell Kam I said goodbye if I don't end up seeing him before I leave."

Otis nods. "Will do."

Coach Becker smiles with a nod, walking off to go tell some of the other alumni his farewell for the evening before heading out. I turn to Otis, wondering if we should do the same. "There's only a few seconds left. Did you want to head out early?"

"It's up to you. We can either wait it out until Kam comes back, or we can leave now to avoid some of the traffic."

I stare at the scoreboard, watching the seconds tick down into nothing as the sound of the buzzer goes off to mark the end of the game. *14-34* was the final score. Harrison lost yet again with no surprise, as the other team won by making another touchdown at the last second.

I turn back to face Otis, shrugging my shoulders. A sigh rolls off of my chest. "I guess we can just wait until the stands clear out, since Kam hasn't made his way back here yet."

Where was he? Where was Kam?

Otis nods in agreement, making his way past me to approach the referee's on the field. He begins talking to one, unsure of what was being said between them as a game ball gets passed in his direction by the other referee.

He catches it, nodding in thanks to them before making his way back over to the tent. He tosses the ball up in the air to himself with each step he makes in my direction.

"No sense in sitting around with nothing to do. How about a few catches back and forth while we wait for Kam?" suggests Otis, tossing the ball in my direction.

I catch it, laughing under my breath. "Knowing Kam, this could go on all night waiting for him to show up."

Otis rolls his eyes, glancing over to the stands to notice most of the home team's side had cleared out. He catches the ball as it's thrown back to him. "I wonder where he went. He's normally not gone for this long."

Where, oh where was Kam?

I glanced over to the concession stands where Otis had mentioned earlier of where he thought Kam was, but there was nobody in sight there. A blank empty area, filled with nothing and nobody but complete darkness.

"Maybe he just headed out to the car to meet up with us later, so he wouldn't have to worry about trying to find us in the crowd of people," says Otis, tossing the ball.

Something wasn't right. Kam wouldn't have just left without telling us where he was going, or if he wanted us to meet up somewhere different later. We all had a plan, and that was to stay put on this field. Nothing else.

I shake my head as I catch the ball for the last time. I pull it into the crease of my upper arm, glancing around with one last hope to spot Kam, still nowhere to be seen.

"He's not here–" I hesitated, leaning over to set the ball onto the ground. I turn to Otis, shaking my head. "He left. He didn't want to be here to begin with, so what reason did he have to stay around here?"

Otis slowly walks up toward me, turning his head over to the entrance of the stadium. A sigh of doubt lets out of him. "Let's just go then."

I nod, making my way over to the remainder of the alumni that was left on the field with Otis to say our goodbyes. It was nice being able to catch up with everyone and that was definitely one of the things I missed since leaving Harrison, seeing all its familiar faces.

Ones that I grew to know all too well, and the ones that I barely got to acknowledge. Bracing their presence day-by-day, never to know the stories behind each and everyone of them. The ones I learned to love, and ones I wanted to hate.

The one that was staring over my every feature. The one who couldn't ever seem to let me go. The one who I desperately wanted to escape with every burning passion in my body.

And there she was, staring back at me.

Brielle Johnston. The girl who didn't want to let me go, no matter what I said and did to her. She'd always find her way back, if that meant into my heart or even my mind.

Chapter Thirty-Two

Brielle

*T*here was no use, absolutely no point at all. No matter how much I searched, I'd never be able to figure him out. Every bit of detail I had believed to have studied was all for nothing, that led up to tonight.

I clench the letter in my hand, letting a sigh of frustration roll out of me. I lean over the fence that surrounded the field on the endzone side, watching Lip laugh underneath the tent. He appeared to be filled with joy as him and Otis passed around the game ball.

My hours of research brought me to this dreaded point, as much as I hated to admit. The passion that burned within had failed me. The one thing I was determined to find had changed without my knowledge.

His car. It wasn't here. The one he drove back in high school, appeared to have changed. It wasn't the same in the way I had planned for this to all play out. In the way my mind wanted it to happen. I was going to leave the letter on his windshield, but I couldn't if the car I remembered wasn't here.

I had to come up with another plan–fast if I still wanted a chance at getting his letter into his hands. It was my only last hope to get this burden off of my chest, once and for all.

Stella and Sadie leaned up next to me, watching the stands clear out as they began to think of another plan.

"You could just not give it to him," suggests Sadie, shrugging her shoulders.

"She has to give it to him. We've made it this far. She has to let him know how these feelings have affected her over the years," demands Stella with confidence in her voice.

I sigh lightly, pulling away from the fence to take a step back. I shake my head, looking toward them. "I have to do it, despite not having a plan from this point forward. I'll come up with something–I always do."

The girls stand silent, hearing the commotion of the passing groups of people leaving as they make their way by us from exiting the stands. Stella's attention shifts to the field with a quick movement in her body, grabbing onto both of our arms to yank us in a different direction.

I turned to glance toward the field, noticing something was different. Lip was gone, and so was

Otis. Where had they gone? Had they left that quickly? Had they noticed me?

"Go—" Stella's voice urges, letting go of my arm, while she still holds onto Sadie's. She smiles with the confidence I was going to need to have. "Go find him. Now!"

A smile tugs on my lips, turning the other direction to begin walking at a faster pace. I hadn't a clue of where he had gone, or where he was going. But I knew I was going to find him, no matter what it took.

I was going to give him this letter...tonight.

My feet hurry through the crowd of people, mending my way through to get toward the entrance of the stadium. The one place I was certain I would find him, that was only if I got there first to stop him from leaving.

I had to do this. I couldn't back out. I had to listen to what my heart was telling me at the moment. That was until it all stopped.

The beating went numb. Frozen with no pulsation. The feeling of when your heart skips a beat without having control of it. The moment of uncertainty placed at your reach, just a few feet away.

There he was. Standing right before me, not focusing in my direction—but he was there.

I had my chance. I could do this—couldn't I?

Lip smiles slightly toward his friends, turning to glance over in my direction in an instant for that smile to fade into nothing. As if it was never a thing to begin with.

Everywhere I looked. I only saw him. Wanting to run. But yet my feet wouldn't move.

Locked looking into his eyes, staring right in my direction. I hadn't a clue what to do.

Run, I told myself.

But I couldn't, nor would I.

Part of myself, filled with a mystery wanting to be uncovered. Yet the other part, wanted it to be left untold to keep myself guessing of all the what ifs.

But here we are, left with fate unfolding at its finest.

My head turns to the side to watch the people surrounding us, feeling all their eyes on us. But they weren't, it was the opposite as they could all care less about us and what was going on. And amongst those people, one caught my eye, staring back in my direction with concern.

Sennedy tilts her head to the side, confused as her eyes don't want to stray away from mine. I hold the letter up in her direction as I smile with a nod, listening to my heart again for what it's always been telling me.

Give the letter to Lip, and don't doubt that this was all meant to happen for a reason.

My eyes trail back to Lip. The beating in my heart raced through my chest with each step taken closer to him.

"Lipton!" my voice calls out.

Maybe this was how our happy ending was supposed to happen. Being placed in this position for a reason with the two of us, in order to confess our love for each other. The chance he was finally going to be able to express his true feelings to tell me he felt the same way back. That he loved me and nothing else.

"*No*. No go away. Please go away–no!" Lip's voice cried out, taking a step back from his friends while holding his hands up defensively.

I hold the letter out for him to grab, beginning to walk after him at a faster pace. *Why was he running?* "Please take this!"

"No. No. No!" his voice continued to cry out, rejecting the letter in my hand. He takes another few steps back, approaching closer to the exit.

"Lip. Lip please!" I begged. *Why was I begging?* "Take this–I need to talk to you–*please*," my voice begins to break with each word spoken. I pushed the letter into his direction. "I'm sorry for everything I did!"

"How about you leave me alone and go back to dealing with your flower bullshit or whatever it is you do for fun, instead of dealing with me. I don't even like you, nor do I want you, and I never will!"

The tears seem uncontrollable, taking another step closer to him. I hadn't a clue in my mind of what was happening and how it was unfolding. All I knew was that I was placed before him, desperate to get him to take this letter, even if I had to beg.

Emotion takes over my mind, without thinking first. The words poured out of me in a cry for help, unsure of why he was acting this way toward me.

I hadn't done anything wrong. I was simply trying to have a conversation with him to get everything off of my chest.

Lip pleads, his hands held up, shaking his head in disbelief. A body sweeps past him to get in the middle of us, within a flash of a second. A flash of his camera light in our direction, with a smirk lining Kam's lips as he holds his phone up to take a photo of Lip and I.

It's like I saw my world change. Flash before my very own eyes.

"Stop, fucking stop it. Quit it!" my voice yells out, anger fuming throughout my body glaring toward Kam's presence. A laugh only follows in his return, as I swing my hand in his direction, attempting to grab the phone out of it.

"Alright–alright. I'll take it. I'll take it. We're good," cries Lip with fear in his tone, glaring back into my eyes that shoot in his direction. He grabs the letter, shoving it into his hoodie pocket.

My eyes quickly dart back in Kam's direction, shaking with fear and the adrenaline running through my veins. Why was I acting like this, so vile in a tone I've never had experienced before?

"You quit it. Now." I demand, taking a step closer to Kam, with no intention of backing down.

"Go away please. No. No. We're good, I'll read it. I'll read it," pleads Lip, still hearing the fear in his voice. He takes a few steps back, Kam and Otis trailing behind him as his eyes never leave mine.

"Please, Lip. Come here!" I begged, slowly approaching him while holding my hand out.

The three of them walk toward the exit of the stadium. Lip doesn't look back as he makes his way down the steps of the entrance. But Kam stops for a second, glancing over his shoulder, showing his endless smirk.

Stella and Sadie slowly make their way up behind me, without saying a word before allowing me to continue on the thoughts and feelings that poured out of me in a way I've never felt.

"You're a fucking dick," my voice yells out. Kam tilts his head to the side, laughing it off and turning away to start walking again. "You're a dick!"

I glance forward to watch them. I slowly begin to walk down the steps of the entrance, never taking my eyes off of them as they walk across the parking lot to make their way to Lip's brand new car.

He never takes the letter out of his pocket, and I wondered why he hadn't. Did he know I was watching and that was why? Or did he really care and was honest that he would read it? But would reading it really mean something to him after the way he just acted toward me?

The three of them get into the car, as Stella makes her way down to where I stood. I glanced over to her, knowing I was able to take my eyes off of them for once after watching them all night.

A sigh lets out of me, allowing another tear to fall with a slight laugh of disbelief. I shake my head at the thought of tonight, and how it all played out in a way I hadn't imagined it to go one bit.

He did it.

It was Kam all along.

He was the one who took those photos back in high school. Made my life a living hell. He was the one who did it all those years ago—*it was him*. Kam did this—but why?

Why did Kam take the photos, and what did he want with them?

What did he want with *me*?

Chapter Thirty-Three

Lipton

I stare at her words, engraved with my name presented on a sealed envelope. But why did she have to go through the trouble of getting it to me exactly?

Especially in the way it happened, acting out in a way I've never seen her. Almost allowing the part of the limerence she had to get to her–that I never imagined could happen to a girl like Brielle.

"Don't just sit there. Open it!" demanded Kam from the passenger seat.

I glance over my shoulder, turning to Otis, who leaned up from the backseat to prop his elbows on the center console. A curious smile pierced through his lips as well to wonder what the letter said.

"Open it. Open it. Open it," the two of their voices began to chant in a pressuring tone.

A sigh lets out of my chest. I begin to tear away the envelope, unsure of the words that lie within. My hands come to a halt halfway through the tear, regretting the thoughts that would come with reading her words–especially around these two.

"No—" my voice hesitated, tossing the letter down onto my lap. "I can't read her words—I can't bring her the satisfaction she thinks she deserves."

Kam snags the letter quickly out of my lap, not giving my reflexes enough time to grab it first. He tears open the rest of the envelope, pulling the letter out to begin reading it aloud.

"*Dear Lipton*—" his voice sympathetically speaks in a pity tone. He flips over the multiple pages filled with words. "What the hell, this bitch really wrote a lot."

I yank it out of his hand, to read it over myself before handing it back to him and then Otis. Another sigh lets out of me, thinking of the words she wrote.

There was nothing wrong with them. She had feelings, just like everyone else and that was something these two couldn't see for some reason.

Brielle wrote the way she was feeling—or the way she's felt, that I've never realized that what we had in high school meant so much to her.

Especially after the way I just treated her...in front of everyone she knew—everyone *I* knew.

I can't imagine how she's feeling, or what's going through her mind. I shouldn't have acted that way. But for some reason I wanted to tell myself that it had to be done that way to get her off of my back.

To please my friends for what they've always wanted me to believe–what they've always wanted done to better myself.

Brielle had to go. I had to sweep her under the rug, as if she never meant a thing to begin with. As Kam would put it, I had to let the bitch go.

"So what are you going to do?" asks Otis, glancing over in my direction.

"He's going to do nothing!" interrupts Kam, leaning back in the passenger seat. "So what? She wrote out her feelings, that doesn't mean anything to us."

My smile fades, not allowing my emotions to get the better of me. Not letting them think of her. "Let's just call it a night. Let her emotions go, and hopefully after tonight. We will never see her again."

Hopefully, is what I could keep trying to promise myself. But this was a small town, so that could be impossible.

*T*he car door shuts in Kam's exit. Otis peers between the front seats to glance over in my direction as I shift the car back into drive.

"Why did you act that way toward Brielle tonight?" he asks with concern in his voice.

I roll my eyes. I keep asking myself the same damn question, Otis. Believe me I do.

"Because I had to. She would continue on with her obsession if I didn't give her a reason to stop it. I had to make her want to leave me alone with the words I used, even if they came out harshly," I softly spoke, staring at the road.

"There's no doubt about it that everything you said was harsh. She didn't deserve any of it, despite what she may have done in your past. You shouldn't have acted that way toward her, Lip."

But it had to be done that way.

"Do I regret it? No. She caused my life to become a living hell, and I won't forget that. It's because of her that I don't have the college career I've dreamed of having–" I begin to rant, waving my hand around.

"No it's not, Lip–it's not Brielle's fault," interrupts Otis, speaking in a firmer tone than usual.

"How so?" I laugh. "How is this all not Brielle's fault? The girl is the definition of insane after the way we all just saw her act tonight. I wouldn't put it past her. I believe she's behind all this to allow my downfall."

"It's not Brielle's fault," he repeats with a break in his voice. "It's someone else's–"

The car pulls into Otis' driveway. I turn in my seat to stare back in his direction, putting the car in park to wait for the words to make their way out of his mouth.

Speak, Otis. Speak.

"It doesn't matter–it's not my place to say," he stutters, reaching for the door handle with panic.

I quickly lock the door, wanting to hear what he has to say. Where was he going with his point?

"If it's not Brielle, then who was it?" I ask, shaking my head in disbelief. "Is it just nobody like every time we get to this part of an argument? Is this one of your ploys to make me believe some nonsense you can come up with? I'm done with this, Otis."

He tugs on the door handle, hoping it would magically unlock. He sighs, shooting a glare in my direction. "It's not a ploy, Lip. She didn't do this to you, and you need to believe she's a good person deep down. She wouldn't want to hurt you!"

I roll my eyes. "I know good people when I see them, and Brielle isn't one of them. All she's done is hurt me and will continue to if I allow her to be in my life. The only good people I have in my life are you and Kam–"

"It was him. It was Kam! He did it!" Otis cries out in a frantic tone. *What was he talking about?* "All those years ago, he did it. He posted the photos and had me take them when I didn't want to, but he pressured me. Then tonight, he did it again. He got involved when he shouldn't have to take another photo. He doesn't want you guys together!"

I stare at him, blinking. Once. Twice. A confused look fills my face, gathering my thoughts into the words he spoke.

Kam took the photos? There was no way–he was my best friend and he had no reason to ruin my life. I knew he disliked Brielle for the most part, but that gave him no reason to ruin her life as well.

I unlock the door, allowing my head to fall into my hand. I had no words. Otis had to be wrong, and it made me sick to think he could come up with this type of story to make me want to turn against my friend.

Kam was innocent. He was misunderstood. But he was never a monster to do such an absurd thing that Otis wanted to paint him out to be.

But I had no way to prove this.

"Get out–" I hesitate, as it's the only words that seem to cross my thoughts at the moment. He grabs onto the handle again, pushing the car door open to get out. He slams it shut behind him without saying another word to follow.

I watch him walk up his driveway, making his way into the house. A sigh of frustration lets out of me, glancing over to the passenger seat in which Kam sat earlier. My eyes followed down the seat to notice he had left his phone charger behind.

I reach out, grabbing onto it to lightly place it down into the cup holder with an idea in mind as I shift the car into reverse to pull out of Otis' driveway.

I think it was time to pay Kam a visit, to get this all straightened out, if for some reason Otis was right about all of this and his assumptions toward Kam's past. To wonder what else Kam could be hiding from the lies he held within that I thought I knew.

Chapter Thirty-Four

Kam

*H*er words were immature, a hopeless romantic at heart. That's everything Brielle was, and in my mind, I don't think I'll ever be able to understand her.

I couldn't understand her not wanting to leave Lip alone. In the reason of her not willing to let the past she shared with him go.

She needed to grow up and face reality.

Not everything is meant to be a bullshit fairytale type of relationship that ends with a happily ever after.

The car door shuts behind my exit of Lip's car, approaching up my driveway toward the house. My fake smile fades into despair as I stand before the front door, wondering what kind of chaos lies behind it, filled with uncertainty.

I reach out, pushing the door open to be met with complete silence. Nobody was here. Not a single soul. I slowly make my way throughout the living room, stepping over the mess my parents had made, that looked like a tornado had run its course through here.

God they needed to clean up.

"Anybody home?" my voice shouts, peering throughout the house to check every room.

There wasn't a trace of anyone, which came as a relief, but also a wonder in my mind to question where everyone had gone. It wasn't like them to have left without a reason, or to at least leave a clue of where they went so late in the evening.

But did I really care? No. I hated them. This was my chance to enjoy my life for once, without them trailing behind me in my own house to judge every single thing I did throughout it.

I couldn't stand them.

I needed to get out of this place as soon as possible. To escape the one thing I've needed to get out of my whole life, and to have the life of freedom I deserved.

No. More. Abuse.

I couldn't take it any longer.

I needed to get out and this weekend was my chance at starting a new life. For the better.

A sigh lets out of me, picking up some of the trash off of the floor and setting it off to the side, to make a clear walkway to my room. I enter my bedroom, tossing my phone down onto the bed and heading straight to the closet to pull out a suitcase.

I hadn't a clue of where I was going or where I was going to end up. All I knew was that I needed to get out of this hellhole sooner than later.

I toss the suitcase down onto my bed, unzipping it and turning back to the closet to grab handfuls of clothing to pack. I needed to take as much as I could, knowing I wasn't planning on returning back here to get the remainder of my stuff that was left behind.

I had to take just enough to survive, uncertain of where my life would end up.

Was I scared? A little–but I would manage. I always do. I always figure a way around things, no matter how hard it got sometimes. I would still be strong and get through this.

I always did. It's what my momma would've wanted. She always wanted the best in life for me. I would do this for her, to better myself.

The suitcase is nearly filled with clothing as I zip it up, tightly securing everything with a sigh of relief. I make my way over to my dresser to begin pulling out the essentials, tossing them onto the bed next to the suitcase to fit in its front pockets.

My mind frantically in a hurry to get my bags packed before they return home, afraid of confrontation about the decision that was made. As they would imply this was all my fault, and they were never to blame. To proclaim this is what I wanted, and what had to be done.

But it was them who told me to leave, and it was what I wanted.

To better myself. This had to be done.

I had to leave, escape this place I once called home.

I toss the suitcase onto the ground, packed and ready to go, wheeling it over toward the door to prop up for my Sunday departure. Another sigh lets out, glancing over at my room at what I'd be leaving behind.

It was all memories. Faded ones at that. Ones that were black and brought regret when looking back at them. I had to leave it behind in order to start fresh.

My eyes make their way over to the nightstand I stood next to, reaching out to grab the plates that were stacked a few inches high from the nights I hid away to eat my dinner alone in my room. The nights that were filled with misery of wondering if I'd be cornered against the wall just one more time within that week over something I had done.

I never deserved any of this—nobody did.

I grasp onto the plates, making my way to the kitchen as I set them into the sink to rinse each one of them off to place into the dishwasher afterwards, while my mind begins to wander. The thoughts that trailed, which seemed never ending.

In my mind I always wanted to wonder where my life would've ended up if I was never placed here. Would I have been raised better, or would every family have treated me the same because I was adopted? I was an outsider in their eyes to not be seen as a person just as they were.

I wonder if for some reason I would've been happier somewhere else. Would I have become a different person to not act in the uncalled ways that I have? Would I not allow myself to get jealous as easily as I did when I would see others living their lives happily?

And it all leads back to that questionable doubt I never wanted to face after tonight. The words she wrote, I could make fun of hundreds of times and I wonder to myself why. Why would I do that—*was it jealousy?* Did somewhere in my mind make me want to act out of spite to cause havoc for what I couldn't have?

To wonder if everything I did to Brielle back in high school, and even tonight, involving her with Lip even more—was all for a reason I couldn't seem to understand. *I wasn't jealous*, I would tell myself. But they had everything I've always wanted for myself. I never wanted to admit the defeat of living in their sorrows.

I was vulnerable to the pain. The heartbreak. The feeling of wanting to be seen, and the feeling of disbelief to know I could ever feel such a thing.

But when I stared into her eyes, all those years ago on the night of prom, that was the one true time that I felt like I was heard. I felt as if I was seen by someone who could have felt the same pain that I shared.

When her eyes looked into mine, I never wanted to look away. There was something about Brielle as much as I hated to admit, I wanted to not like her. But my heart wanted to continue beating for every breath she took. A girl I'm supposed to hate, but for some reason I can't.

God, what has she done to me?

I tense my shoulders, allowing the thoughts to go back as they once were. I take a deep breath, standing straight up as the last plate is set into the dishwasher. I stare out the kitchen window that's above the sink, noticing something in the distance.

Not something. *Someone.* A dark shadow of a figure who is staring back in my direction.

Chapter Thirty-Five

Brielle

"*W*e'll take two vanilla ice cream cones please."

Stella's ideas weren't always the grandest, unless it meant coming down to fixing a problem with ice cream while we talked it over, then they were worth listening to.

A smile twists its way onto my lips. I glance over to see her body filling the passenger seat of my car as she holds a five dollar bill in my direction.

"I got this. It's the least I could do after everything that happened tonight," she says. A sincere smile piercing her lips, taking the five from her.

I pull through the drive-thru to approach the window to pay and collect our ice cream cones. I pass Stella's over to her as I quickly take a lick of mine to prevent it from dripping onto my lap, while pulling into a parking spot.

I shift the car into park, leaning back into my seat to glance over in Stella's direction. My thoughts were everywhere and I couldn't seem to get them straight after what happened. A tiny laugh lets out of me, replaying the night over.

I just didn't understand it. Understand *him*.

"Thanks," I eventually say to her in a soft spoken tone. It's the only words I seem to be able to find at the moment.

Stella nods, leaning back in her seat. She props her back against the door, while pressing her feet up to the center console. She stares toward me, taking a lick of her ice cream. "It didn't have to happen that way tonight."

Believe me Stella, I've thought the same thing. Wished for the same thing–over and over again.

"But he took the letter–" I laughed with an uneasy tone. "I thought it would have been simpler. But just like every time, he allows his friends to get the better of him. Turn him into this person he isn't."

"Bre–he took the letter. He wanted to hear what you had to say. If he didn't want to take it, he could have just walked away without saying a word. But yet, he stood there and listened. He may have not said what you wanted to hear at the moment. But Lip still looked you in the eyes and saw the hurt that came with them. So he took the letter to show you that he still cared."

I roll my eyes, laughing under my breath. "That he still cared? He hasn't cared about me in a long time, Stella! And if for some reason he did care, he wouldn't have said those hurtful things to me!"

Stella takes another lick of her ice cream, leaning forward with a puzzled expression. She had no clue of anything Lip said to me. She hadn't realized how badly his words hurt, they felt like a knife digging into my heart for all the things I could've felt about him.

Everything he said played back in my mind. The hurt and break with every word spoken, repeated over and over again, like an old tape recorder that I could never turn off. His words scarred into the folds of my mind to never forget.

"He told me *no*. He told me to *go away*. It wasn't until I had to beg him to take the letter that he finally listened–or until he saw another side of me. It all appears to be a blur in my mind, even though it was just a few hours ago. But when Kam came up, something changed within me to react in an unmindful way toward them both. Anger in one aspect. Pity in another. Both completely different," I add, shaking my head.

Stella places her hand on mine, glancing into my eyes with sympathy. "He still took the letter, didn't he?" I nod, unsure of where her point was going. "He must still care even if he didn't show it. He took the letter for a reason we may never be able to understand."

A smile twists its way onto my lips, taking the last bite of my ice cream. I adjust myself in my seat before placing my hand onto the joystick to shift the car into drive. The sound of my phone notification stops me in my tracks.

Stella and I shot each other a look, questioning if this was fate unfolding at its finest. If for some odd reason he had chosen to make contact this quickly. I reach down to grab my phone out of the cupholder to reveal that wasn't quite so.

But instead there sat an unread message from Sennedy. I opened the message to reply.

Sennedy Marie

Sennedy: 9:47 P.M.
So you gave Lip a letter...
It all makes sense now.
The flash of paper earlier.
That was the letter.

Me: 9:48 P.M.
What letter?
I didn't give Lip anything.

Sennedy: 9:48 P.M.
(Image File)
This has your name written all over it.

Me: 9:48 P.M.
So what. I wrote him a letter.
I was expressing my feelings.

Sennedy: 9:49 P.M.
Yeah, I could tell.
More like I could see, thanks to Kam.

Me: 9:49 P.M.
What do you mean, see?

Sennedy: 9:50 P.M.
The photos of you and Lipton.
From tonight.
They're everywhere.
Same with the letter.
Everyone knows.

I toss my phone down onto the floorboard, leaning back in my seat to stare at the ceiling. I run my hands through my hair, beginning to laugh in disbelief.

This. Couldn't. Be. Real.

I shake my head, screaming to myself on the inside as I shift the car into gear to drive out of the parking lot. Stella glances over in my direction without

285

a word to say the entire car ride back to drop her off at her place.

My thoughts are trailing. Spiraling. Nonstop of all the unimaginable things that came out of tonight, that started out of nothing. The endless possibilities of what could come next if I allowed these rumors to continue to build into something new, that wasn't just a wildfire that could be put out as easily as before.

This was stronger. This was bolder. This was unbearable.

I couldn't stand for it, and no matter how fast my foot hit this gas pedal, there was nothing stopping me. Nothing that could get in my way to put an end to this disaster that should've been done a long time ago.

This was caused by Kam.

And nothing was going to stop me from putting an end to his nonsense. Putting him in his place, that nobody realized needed to be done a long time ago.

He needed an end put to him.

But no matter how fast I drove. I'd make sure I'd make it to him. Make him pay for what he's done to me–for the pain he's caused, I'd make him feel it. For everything he did to Lip. For everything he's done to *me*. I'd make sure it was the last thing I would do, no matter how much it hurt him, or me.

I'd make Kam suffer, just like he made everyone else suffer.

Chapter Thirty-Six

Brielle

"*W*ho's out there?" Kam's voice questions in the distance, hearing the door shut behind him. He really hadn't a clue.

I stared over his figure, allowing the laugh to fall that only I could hear, that it appeared to be just the two of us under the dark of the night sky.

"Took you long enough," I scolded, taking a step closer to him. He couldn't see who was standing before him yet. A smile pierced my lips, approaching him. "Quite a nice place you have here."

Kam slowly walked in my direction, the only light surrounding us was the back porch light and the faded light from the street lamps.

He tilts his head to the side, shaking it in disbelief as he catches a glimpse of my red hair. "Brielle–" he laughs to himself. "I should've known it was you. Quite the night we had tonight, wasn't it?"

I clench my fist, nearly feet away from him as I come to a halt to stare him down. Quite the opposite, Kam–wouldn't you like to know?

"Your letter to Lip was sweet–too sweet it appeared it may have made you bitter and cold hearted," he adds, laughing under his breath.

He takes a few more steps forward, getting closer by the second. Temptation to just put an end to him was strong. But I had to hold out. Had to hear him out.

"Don't," my voice cuts, stronger than it should've. I take a step closer, glaring at him. "Don't mention his name when all you've done is turn against him when he's supposed to be your best friend!"

Kam's laugh is hysterical, sounding as if he could be choking on it. "My best friend? Lip didn't mean a thing to me, Brielle! I used him to have a place to be seen, until I got what I wanted. Revenge for my voice to be heard, and others to be hurt."

I shake my head to question his words. *He used Lip...to be seen and heard–but why?* What could Kam possibly want out of all of this to cause such vengeance to those around him.

"He *is* your friend, Kam. You can't say he isn't when all Lip has done is be there for you. The same goes for Otis. The two of them care about you, despite you not showing the same affection back. They're still your friends at the end of the day."

Kam rolls his eyes in the glimpse of light I can see. He takes another step forward to kick at the dirt, glaring back into my eyes. His piercing gaze is mesmerizing with all the lies held behind them.

"Brielle, what do you want?" he hissed. Annoyance painted all over him. "You show up at my house unannounced with no reason to give exactly why, simply just after the bad night it appears you may have had tonight."

I inch closer to him, wondering how much closer we could possibly get. I roll my eyes without a care of how annoyed he may have felt with my presence just randomly showing up unannounced on this late Friday night.

"You should have asked that question of what I wanted a long time ago," my voice demands, pointing my finger in his face. My body furiously fuming with every step taken to get closer to him, uncertain of what I could do out of anger. "The photos that you took–I wanted those gone. But every time when I thought I was just about to escape, another one showed up. Then tonight, it all came clear. It was you. You took those damn photos!"

A laugh slips out of Kam, nodding his head in agreement. He clearly was admitting what he had done, but showed no mercy to have regretted it. The way I was feeling didn't seem to bring him any sympathy.

"But I'm asking you now, Bre. What do you want? You want those photos gone, you could've just asked." A smirk makes its way to his lips, as he seems to be lost in the stare he holds to me. "I took the photos, so what? What are you going to do about it?"

What am I going to do about it? What could I do?

There wasn't anything that could bring me enough satisfaction to clear what has already been done in the past, and nothing that could lead on after today to have a brighter future with how everything had unfolded.

Anger tenses through my veins, clenching my fist as my mind falls free of any of the thoughts telling me to think otherwise from this point forward. My hands in a swift movement collide into Kam's chest, forcing his body down onto the ground. I take a step forward, standing over him as he stares up at my figure.

His back flat on the ground as his hands tremble against the dirt, attempting to pull himself back up. He kicks his knees back in a way of defense, watching him struggle to get back up in a hurry.

He's too weak.

"What am I going to do?" I laugh, rolling my eyes once more. I press one of my feet onto his abdomen, while the other one presses down onto his hand that's held at his side, with just enough pressure to make it hurt. "I should be asking myself the same thing."

Kam glares at me, wincing at the pain as he bares his teeth, without any words to fall as I watch the sorrow wash over him. He didn't seem scared. But he should be after I'm through with him.

My foot twists down into his hand, forcing the pain to unleash within him, bringing a smile to my lips, watching him break as he begins to feel the pain.

I was hurting him. *Good.* And he felt it, even better.

My voice trickles into a soft laugh. "That's the dreaded question I should've been asked years ago. What do I want?" My eyes roll, allowing the smile to widen. "The things I could've had and the things that could've been done. We're a lot more alike than we both want to realize, Kam."

He coughs out a laugh of disbelief with a roll of his eyes before attempting to pull himself up. But I force his body to stay down. He lies there pitifully, staring back into my eyes.

"That's why I'm asking you now. To get a better understanding of you. To wonder how you believe that we're alike in some sort of messed up way," he winces with a grind of his teeth. "Nobody can have a past as painful as mine."

I release my feet from both his abdomen and hand, to take a step back to stare over at him. My body begins to tense with nerves, allowing my head to fall into my hands with a laugh of disbelief that he could be this naive.

My past was painful. One I very rarely shared, that not even Stella or Halle knew about. A past that consisted of many different things that built me into the person I am today. And maybe in some sort of way that past had built me into the way I grew today, to not allow Lip to go so easily as I had let everyone else go from my past.

"You and I are alike, Kam," my voice bitterly laughs. I take a small step toward him with a tilt of my head. "Pain or not. We both have felt the same thing in different ways. The feeling of neglect when it was the time that we both needed someone to be there for us the most."

Kam slowly presses his hands against the dirt to pull himself up. I allow it–for now. He leans back on his hands, tilting his head to the side, appearing to be as lost as a puppy.

"And your point is?" he dryly questions.

I kneel down in front of him, brushing my hand along his jawline to tilt his attention up in my direction.

"My past was filled with pain, and you being in it doesn't seem to make it any better," I scoffed. My hand guides down to his chest to nudge him back. "When I was younger, I thought my life was going to be simple. But things aren't always what they appear to be. My mom worked during the days, and my dad worked during the night. So it was very rare that I got to spend time with either one of them, and as a young child that was a hard thing to understand."

Kam nods at my words, staying down and not bothering to pull himself back up. I wasn't sure if he understood my point, but he was listening to every word I spoke.

A smile twists its way onto my lips to carry on my words. "With the passion of neglect, it allowed me to grow to trust new things. A passion of hate grew into something new. Something stronger. Something that no matter how many times it could die, it would still come back. The passion for flowers became the only thing I allowed my mind to trust. Because as many times as a flower would bloom over the seasons, it would always come back, unlike my parents and the care they lacked to give. And in those years, as my parents became distant, they began to not care any more as I got older. They realized I could live on my own without any care. So in my mind, I became just like a flower. I could bloom to become beautiful and peaceful, or I could bloom to grow one day to have thorns, to cause hurt for the same pain I've felt over the years."

I pull my hand back from him, to stand to my feet. I roll my eyes, laughing under my breath. He stares at me, lost in my words. I wonder to myself if he wants to reply, or simply what was going through his mind with what I had said, as now he could see me in a different perspective from the girl he once knew.

Tonight changed me. It changed me in a lot of ways I'm not willing to understand quite yet. Tonight was meant to have peace and a perfect understanding, with a happy ending that I hoped to have. But instead, it brought anger and regret, that was filled with an ending of uncertainty from this point forward.

"Bre–I'm sorry you had to go through that," his voice finally speaks. His tone doesn't come across as sincere and it makes me wonder if he's actually sorry.

I cough out a laugh, pressing my foot back into his abdomen. It should've never left there in the first place. I glare down at him. "You're. Not. Sorry." He rolls his eyes in response. "If you were sorry, you never would've hurt Lip or I with everything you've done!"

"I didn't mean to hurt you–" he cries out in pain as my foot presses harder against him.

"But you meant to hurt Lip?" I ask, shaking my head. "Everything you've done in the past, regardless if he was your friend or not. He was still a person *you* hurt. *I* was still a person you hurt. And it all makes me wonder why. Why did you do all of this if you never meant to hurt us?"

Kam's stare is blank as he runs his hand through his hair. There's words he wants to say, I can tell. But for some reason he doesn't speak of them aloud. His lips fall open, biting nervously at them.

"Kam–what is it?" *Why should I care?* Why should I care about him, when all he's done is hurt me? "You know how you feel–about everything?"

"I'm only falling in love with you, Brielle." The words cut out of him like a knife to the heart with the regretful tone he speaks. "And the truth is. The more I am, the more it hurts me."

I stared at him, wondering where all of this was coming from. Was this why he had done everything he has, simply out of jealousy over the years?

He sighs out a laugh, possibly wondering to himself where this sudden confession was coming from. "I want to love you. But I can't. Because loving you will only hurt me more when I have to lose you. Lose you in the end to him."

Lose you in the end to him? Was he afraid for some reason that my feelings about Lip and the way I've always felt about him would allow me to slip into this void to not realize how Kam felt about the situation?

His words confused me. *He loved me.* But in my heart I hated him. Those were feelings that couldn't mix. Not after everything he's done to me. He's hurt me. He's hurt Lip. And most of all, he's hurt there being an *us* from ever happening.

Kam inches his body forward, baring his teeth from the pain as he pushes himself against my foot. I don't budge as I shake my head at the thought of his words that can't seem to leave my mind.

"Don't–" I harshly say. I force my foot down harder against his strength. He tries to push back. "Don't try to make another move–"

A smirk piercing through his lips, not bothering to listen to the words I kindly asked of him. His strength becomes stronger, knocking my body down onto the ground in a swift movement of his hands. He slowly pulls himself up onto his knees with a sigh of relief.

I lay there, glaring deeply into his eyes that now stare over me. I clench my fist with every muscle in my body, with the tempting urge to not want to fight back against him. As the feeling doesn't last longer than a few seconds, springing to stand upright.

"I said don't make another move!" It's more of a command than anything. I glare down at him, still with his knees pressed against the dirt. He stares back, laughing under his breath, tilting his head at the demands I make. A gentle laugh slips past my lips. "You just don't listen, do you?"

My words don't seem to phase him as he's already trying to make another move. He couldn't say that I didn't warn him because I didn't come to play nice.

"I said don't make another move!" my voice yells out. I quickly scurry across the dirt to grab the nearest object, which happens to be a baseball bat. I swing it in his direction with all of my force as Kam slowly attempts to rise to his feet. But instead he's knocked back down onto the ground, hearing the bat colliding with his skull.

I hold the bat over my shoulder, glaring down at him. Adrenaline running through my veins as he lies there with blood beginning to trickle down the side of his face as he glares back into my eyes.

He was still alive. *Great.*

His hand traces up to the blood, running his fingers over it. He pulls his shaky hand back to stare deeply at the blood. Shock fills his face. "Wh–what did you do?"

What did I do? What was I doing?

"Don't move and I'll make this easy," I softly say. I pull the bat off of my shoulder to press it into the dirt to lean over onto it. A smile continues to tug its way onto my lips and it has me wondering why after everything I've done.

Was I enjoying this? Watching him suffer? Knowing he was finally feeling the pain I've felt all these years because of him?

"Brielle–*don't*–" his voice attempts to speak. His blood covered hand reaching out in my direction as a plea of defeat. "Don't do this. You'll regret it."

I want to believe his words. But I know everything he says is only to better himself in the situation he desperately wanted to get out of. He didn't enjoy this, as much as I did. He didn't like being the center of attention for everything wrong he's done.

He enjoyed having others suffer just so he could thrive. But now that he was placed in a position, he didn't seem to like it the other way around.

My glare is strong. Intimidating. Staring back at him with no regrets that he feels I might have. A laugh trickles its way up my throat with a tilt of my head. "I don't regret this. It's what has to be done."

I swing the bat over my shoulder, rolling my neck once to release the nerves I was feeling. And with no regrets, no remorse, I began to swing it over and over again in his direction, making sure each hit to him drew even more blood than the last.

When I'm finished, a sigh of relief lets out of me, dropping the bat down to my side as I stare over Kam's dead body that bleeds out onto the ground underneath him. A smirk of satisfaction grows on my lips, to know I had finally put an end to his nonsense.

He was no more. Kam was dead. Because of me.

And I couldn't be happier.

"Goodbye, Kam," my voice laughs, turning my body in the other direction.

I slowly trail across the backyard, with the bat in hand, hiding and clearing any evidence that I was ever here. I couldn't be caught for this murder. Nobody would understand why I did it. Maybe not even Lip could bring himself to understand it. I toss the bat over the fence into the neighbor's yard as I let out another sigh and this time it's the feeling of satisfaction that brushes over me.

There were no more worries. My life could finally get back on track in the way I've always wanted it. I had the closure I needed to have once and for all. I could finally start fresh again.

And maybe, just maybe there could still be a chance for a relationship between Lip and I to happen without Kam standing in the way anymore.

I was beginning to have hope for the two of us.

The smile I couldn't seem to get rid of tugs at my lips as I reached for the handle of my car door that was parked along the street. The handle was stuck and it wouldn't budge. My hands quickly begin to rummage in all of my pockets, clueless of where my keys could have gone.

They were missing–I must have dropped them in the backyard. *Shit.*

"You've got to be kidding me!" I sighed, tilting my head up to the dark night sky. I tug on the handle again, hoping the outcome would be different. But it's still locked. "Great. Just great!"

I quickly glance around, hoping nobody is near to be watching me as I attempt to make my way to the backyard to scavenge for my car keys. What I had hoped for didn't come as easily. A set of headlights makes its way down the road at a slow pace, right in my direction.

With all the regrets that I swore I wouldn't have, those regrets begin to fill my nerves and twist my stomach into knots. Just with that hope to pray they aren't headed anywhere near here any time soon.

Chapter Thirty-Seven

Lipton

If all of this was true, I couldn't be his friend anymore.

I clench Kam's phone charger in my hand against the steering wheel with the drowning sound of the music playing over the radio in the background. My emotions were stirring inside of me, still not sure of how to feel about this entire situation.

Part of me felt that it was wrong to accept what Kam had done to Brielle and I, if for some reason it happened to be true about what Otis had said. As the other part was telling me to let him go, knowing deep down if Kam did it once, what was going to stop him from doing it again.

I couldn't have someone in my life, especially a friend who would turn their backs so easily on me, when they should be someone I should be able to trust. And that's what I thought Kam was, someone who wouldn't turn against me, when all I've been able to do is trust him after everything he's been through.

Kam didn't have the best life. But that didn't make him a monster.

He had to be innocent.

He had to be. I just knew it.

The music fades into silence as I allow many other thoughts to take over my mind during the drive, dwelling back on the night and what came out of it.

There was a lot I couldn't seem to be able to put into words. The emotions I wasn't able to express how badly they hurt me until I realized it was too late. The pain of this burden I held onto for so many years, not willing to let it go.

As many times as Kam's words would twist into my mind of what he thought was best, I finally started to listen with the hope of bringing myself clarity from what I've longed to escape. Her painful eyes that would stare back at me for what felt like an eternity, and that shade of her hair that burned as bright as a fire.

Brielle would become my weakness, only if I allowed her to. So I had to bring myself to realize that one thing. It was better to let her go, than if I continued to hold onto her any longer.

She would become the death of me.

My hand gently brushes down the steering wheel as I let all of my thoughts go. My eyes stray ahead back onto the road, rounding the corner to drive down Kam's street. A sigh falls from my chest, unsure of how to feel in this situation.

There were so many things I wanted to say if this was true. So many things I wanted to begin questioning over what he's done in the past. But in my heart, I wanted to see and believe he would never do anything to hurt me.

He wouldn't do that to me. I had to believe that.

In the years I have known Kam, I have always been there for him when he's needed it the most. And the same went for when I needed him the most, he was there no matter what.

During every game and practice of the season. He was there. During every failure and success I had. He was there. During every up and down we had in our lives. We were still there for each other at the end of it.

There was nothing anyone could say that would tear my friendship away from Kam.

He needed me just as much as I needed him.

The memories of the past I shared with him begin to trace over my mind, tugging a smile onto the corner of my lips. Every memory I shared with Kam was better than the last, and I never wanted to forget them.

He was my best friend. I never wanted to lose him.

The smile on my lips slowly begins to fade back into nothing, approaching Kam's house, to drive down his street that was only lit by dull street lamps. My eyes remain straight on the road to notice something stopped up ahead.

I glance down at the time on the clock. It was a little after eleven. My hand trails down to grab my phone out of the cupholder, keeping a far distance from what lies ahead. I begin to dial out to an emergency dispatch, placing the phone to my ear.

"*911*, what's your emergency?" the voice over the phone speaks.

"There's something ahead in the road." I squint my eyes in the dull light, hoping to get a better glance. "It's either a deer...maybe a person. I'm not sure."

"Are there any signs of movement?"

I lean forward over my steering wheel. I glance around as something else catches my eye. "There's a car parked on the side of the road. No headlights. But there's someone outside of it, appearing to be pacing around."

"What's your location?" I tell them Kam's address. "Someone will be out there shortly. Stay where you are, and don't approach the scene."

The phone hangs up, setting it back down into my cupholder. I stared ahead, curious about what was going on. It was too late for someone to be out at this time of night, especially on the side of the road in the middle of nowhere.

Something wasn't right.

I had to check it out.

I slowly inch off of the break, lightly pressing the gas to drive closer to Kam's house. My vision becomes clear, grabbing a glimpse of the person standing outside of the parked vehicle. Her red hair flowing down past her shoulder in the moonlight.

Brielle. Why was she here?

I drive up behind her car, shifting it into park and turning off my ignition. I dragged myself out of the car for a mere second to make sure she was alright. At this moment, I didn't care what happened between us tonight. I just wanted to make sure she was okay.

Her glare quickly shoots in my direction, unsure if she was startled or disgusted by seeing me after everything. I approach her without any words to follow, studying over her appearance.

She looked relieved, yet intimidated for some reason.

"Wh-what are you doing here?" her voice stutters in an uneasy tone.

I hold up Kam's phone charger. "He left it in my car, so I had to return it." She nods, trailing her eye contact away from me. I glanced over her to know something was off. "I should be asking you the same thing. Why are you here?"

She slowly turns back, tilting her head to the side as she crosses her arms against her chest. A smile tugs at her lips. "No reason–"

My hand reaches out to touch the side of her tilted face, tugging it in my direction. My thumb brushes over a red mark on her cheek that runs down to her jawline. *Blood.* Warm fresh blood coated along her skin.

I pull my hand back from her cheek, to stare at the blood coating my fingers. I glance up in her direction, watching that tempting smile never fade from her lips.

"I need to see Kam," I quickly said in a hurry. I don't question her on the blood. I just let it go for now, pushing her aside.

My feet race against the dirt, making my way into the front yard of his house. Brielle's feet follow close behind, attempting to keep up with my fast pace. Why was she following me? What did she want?

I take a step onto the porch as I extend my hand out to grab for the door handle. Brielle's feet come to a halt at the same time as mine, standing at a far distance away. I wanted to turn over my shoulder to watch her. Wonder what she was doing here. But I didn't have time for that. I needed to talk to Kam. Now.

I clench onto the handle, letting out a sigh at the thought of turning it. But instead, Brielle's words begin to fill my mind. She speaks at a tone I've never heard from her before. A tone that comes across as a demand, or a tone that sounds as simple as she could be asking.

"Don't," that's the only word she speaks, grabbing onto my wrist to yank back in her direction.

Chapter Thirty-Eight

Brielle

I never wanted to hurt him. But here we are, yanking him down onto the ground with all of my force at my command.

Lip's eyes dart in my direction, too stunned to want to look at me. But he still does. There's a taunting haze that beams within them. A gentle stare held in a way I've never seen him look at me before. In a way I never wanted him to look away.

He tenses his muscles lightly to himself to push his body upward in a steady motion. His stare never leaves mine in every movement made. Every breath taken.

Lip rises to his feet as he flexes out the hand he landed on in front of him, to check if it was alright. A slow breath lets out of him.

"Where is Kam?" It's the only words he allows to fall from his lips, never straying away from any of my movements.

A smile pierced through my lips, taking a step closer to him. He doesn't move, which is a good decision on his end because I wouldn't want him to end up like Kam.

I wouldn't want to have to do that again.

"He's not here." The smile never fades. I inch a step forward, twisting it into a slight laugh as I brush the tips of my fingers against his chest.

Lip shakes his head in somewhat disbelief. He wasn't buying any of this. I could understand why, starting with the fact that he caught me at Kam's house for no apparent reason.

I wasn't friends with Kam. I never was friends with Kam. And I will never be friends with Kam.

"I don't believe that–" Lip lets out a shaky breath as he takes a step back off of the sidewalk with his hands up defensively. My eyes follow his movements as they begin to trail toward the side of the house, inching closer to the backyard.

Shit. *Shit*. Shit.

"Lip wait!" my voice calls out, instantly getting flashbacks to tonight. But instead of running away in the way he had earlier, he actually stops to listen.

He turns around, merely inches away from the side of the house. The exact place where you'd be able to see the silhouette of Kam's body from afar. But I've caught him just in time as I stare over him, clueless of what to say to keep his attention.

"What is it?" he sighs out. His body inches a step back. "I really need to find Kam."

My feet begin to race after him. I grab onto his arm to yank it back in my direction for his eyes to stare into mine. "You can't–you can't find him. Can't go looking for him. I need to talk to you–alone."

I release his arm, watching it fall down to his side as he takes a step closer to me. "I'm all ears, Brielle. Go on with what can't seem to wait a matter of a few minutes."

I steady my breath. Calm my nerves. I stare back into his eyes, not allowing my emotions to fall out of control. A tender, soft smile fills my lips, standing before him.

"He wasn't your friend," I blatantly say. It was nothing but the truth. But would Lip see it that way? "Kam used you, Lip. He used *us* for his own satisfaction."

He begins to shake his head in disbelief as his lips fall open in somewhat shock. "Kam didn't use me–he never would. He's my best friend."

"That's where you're wrong, Lip," my voice cries out. Here comes the emotions. "Those photos that appeared during high school that taunted the both of us. It was because of Kam. Then tonight, he did

312

the same thing. I'm not sure how you don't see what he's done."

Lip turns his head to the side, letting out a soft sigh under his breath. "So Otis wasn't making it up–" His words don't come out clear to me as it appears he was talking to himself more than anything.

I let it go to carry on with my words. "Kam wasn't a good person. He used you until you weren't any good anymore. Everything he did that you may have thought was good, was never out of the kindness of his heart. He didn't have a heart because his heart was broken. And for that reason, he didn't think anyone could be happy."

Lip glanced back toward me, not willing to let a smile tug at his lips over the true words spoken. He grows colder. Bitter with a bark in his tone. "Kam is a good person. Yeah, he may have done some bad things in the past. But that doesn't make him a monster. We all make mistakes!"

His feet slowly start to trail back, approaching the side of the house. And this time, I do nothing to stop him. I allow his feet to take small steps toward what lies ahead, knowing it was a matter of time until he found out the truth.

"We all make mistakes–" I repeat softly. "We all *make* mistakes we have to live with."

The backyard is now in view, as we stand at the side of the house. Lip snaps his focus back in my direction. A confused look possesses it, watching his disbelief turn into a tiny smile tugging at the corner of his lips.

"Where is Kam?" his voice asks, this time in more of a demand. He watches my smile grow immensely as I take a step closer to run my fingers up his chest again. He snaps his head to the side, and the smile fades from his lips. He's spotted the dark outline of the silhouette.

He's spotted Kam.

Lip takes a step in Kam's direction. But my grip is too tight, tugging at his arm to keep his body back. Lip glares over his shoulder, doing all he can to fight against me. He wants to run. But his feet stay flat. He doesn't move.

"Kam–Kam can you hear me!" Lip's voice calls out, waving his hands in the air to grab Kam's attention. But there's no point. Not worth the wasted effort he's putting into this. "It's Lip. I need to talk to you."

Kam's body doesn't budge, which I would hope it wouldn't or else we'd have a problem. I gently let go of Lip's arm, taking a step back, watching his beaming eyes of confusion that build with the wrath of fury.

"What did you do to him?" his voice says in a harsh tone.

"I didn't do anything!" I defensively yell out with my hands up.

Lip glares back in Kam's direction. The look of debate fills his face, wondering if he should take another step. Wondering if it was worth it in his mind to see the uncertainty of lies ahead for his friend.

"You—you kill—killed him—" his voice trembles, taking a step back. I quickly reach out to grab his hand. A moment of reassurance, in his eyes that I was a good person. I could never be a killer to him. He quickly swats my hand away, inching another few steps back.

"I didn't kill him!" I yell out. I even wanted to make myself believe I could never do such a thing. "I didn't kill Kam!"

Lip looks down at his hand. The same one that touched my face earlier when he got here, just a matter of minutes ago. He stares at it for a long second before holding it out in my direction, watching it shake.

Blood. Blood lined his fingers in where he had touched my face with his hands. Not just any blood.

Kam's blood lined his hand. His own friend's blood he had once loved despite what he had done to him.

Kam was still Lip's friend in his eyes. And now he was left to remember him by staring down at the blood that lined his hand. All because of me. He would never forget this.

"You killed him," his voice repeats. He takes another small step back. "You killed Kam."

In my mind, all I wanted to do was scream at the top of my lungs that I didn't do it. I wanted to believe I could never do such a criminal thing to someone. When it all came down to it, I wanted to admit what I had done. Because at the end of the day, Kam had it coming, sooner than later.

"I didn't kill Kam!" my voice continues to plead. I take a step closer to Lip, watching the timid feelings begin to wash over him. "And if I did, think of what this could mean for us," my voice laughs out. "He wouldn't be in the way anymore to ruin that!"

My laugh trickles into a grin. I reach out to grab Lip's hand, tugging it in my direction. I didn't want to let him go. But it was him who was tearing us apart, yanking his hand back to his side.

"Brielle, enough!" he yells. He's too stunned to speak. Too hesitant to allow the words to fall from his lips. "I've had enough. Enough of you. Enough of all of this. And definitely enough to know that there will never be an us!"

I stare over him. His words had to be my mind playing tricks on me. There was no way Lip could give this up. We worked so hard to get to this point. *I worked so hard to get to this point.* The moment I dreamed to have between us was broken into pieces. Shattered glass that could never be repaired.

But that wasn't going to allow me to give up. Not that easily.

The sound of sirens fade in the distance, staring over every one of Lip's features. There was something about him I never wanted to get out of my mind. A dream worth chasing. A nightmare that I could never escape. An ending with him that was worth fighting for, no matter what it took to get there.

But here we stand. Staring into each other's eyes with uncertainty of where the future lies ahead. I killed his best friend. He wouldn't be able to forgive me for that. But I never could admit to it either, knowing how much it would hurt him, hearing those words fall from my lips.

I killed your best friend, Lip. I killed Kam.

The sirens grow louder and in my heart I know I don't have much time to run. I couldn't run when I wanted to prove myself not guilty to Lip. I had to be innocent to the man I wanted to call mine one day. So I halt my feet, keeping my distance as a smile curls onto my lips one last time.

"Believe what you want to. But in my heart I never did it. I never wanted to hurt you," I slowly say, shaking my head to the thought of what I had done. A police car pulls up onto the grass, many officers exit to walk in our direction. Lip points them in the direction of the backyard. "There will always be an us, Lip–"

The officers approach the backyard, gathering the information regarding Kam's death. My ears begin to go hazy, not listening to the growing sound of shouting about what had happened. My sight fixated on Lip, glaring over my presence.

He points his trembling finger in my direction, still not wanting to believe any of this is true. "She did it. She killed Kam–" The words fall from his lips and it's the only thing I hear from him, and it sounds just like my heart was breaking.

I was losing him all over again, and this time, I may have just lost him for good.

My hands are guided to my back with no hesitation. My eyes never want to look away from Lip's. He did this to me. He got me arrested, and there was no turning back for the crime I had done.

Kam was dead. It was all because of me.

And I couldn't be more proud of it.

I stare at Lip, his hands being pulled behind his back to be cuffed as well. He didn't do anything, why was he being arrested?

An expression begins to fill his face, laced with a sense of confusion and disbelief. He didn't understand this either. He wasn't the one who committed the crime.

His voice wanted to plead not guilty in the same way mine had. But he kept his mouth shut, knowing it would be better that way in this situation.

My smile fades, feeling the cuffs tightened and my wrists ache and they become numb with each tug taken toward the police car. I glance over my shoulder, willing to get another glimpse of him.

He didn't want this. I could tell that, but it had to be done.

A hand is pressed against my head as the car door is opened to lower me inside. A smirk piercing through my lips, getting a final tempting glance at the one, who I would one day call mine, being lowered into a different police car.

"Lip, please I didn't do this!" my voice calls out. "You have to believe me!"

He doesn't say a word, watching over his shoulder as my body is fully escorted into the backseat of the police car and the car door is slammed shut.

I stare out the window, feeling that smile turn into a grin with the shake of my head. I didn't do this, is what I would keep telling myself if I wanted to prove myself not guilty to the world.

Plead not guilty to Lip for what we could still have. I wanted to plead my case to Lip a hundred times over until he would believe me. Believe every word I would say. But I knew this wasn't our last time together. He would find his way back to me when he realized what he was truly missing.

The piece of his heart that has always needed to be found to become whole.

That piece that was there all along, that he never wanted to bring himself to realize how much it meant to him to begin with. The part that he would never give up as long as his heart still beats on.

This is what it's come down to, and in those short days after, I never wanted to forget what he had done.

Lip was let go, pleading himself not guilty after the evidence was gathered once brought into the interrogation room. And when mommy and daddy's money was able to buy him out of the situation for him to have no part of it.

I was found guilty. All the evidence led back to me. I had done it.

I couldn't escape this.

I was found guilty for killing Kam. No verdict. No need for an explanation to plead my case that it was self defense.

Nobody cared about the murder's side of the story, that this was all meant to happen for a reason.

To look back at this to realize one thing in my heart. I will do whatever it takes to make sure Lipton Devonshire is mine at the end of it.

Even if it breaks me. Breaks us. Breaks everything from happening in the way it should. It won't stop me from doing anything to make sure he is mine, and nobody else's.

If that meant killing Kam–then so be it. Killing him was only the beginning of our twisted tainted love story. For as long as my heart shall beat on, I will never forget him.

Never forget what we could've had. What we still can have.

Until death would do us part. He will be mine.

No matter what it takes.

Lip will be mine. Even if it's meant to break me in the process, watching him through bars, having everything I wished we could've had. Together as the whole we will one day be, as long as we both shall live.

Epilogue

Lipton

3 Weeks Later

*I*t took weeks for Otis and I to convince Kam's parents to have a service for him. And when we finally did, we were the ones left to plan it, due to his parents' constant state of grieving over his loss.

It took a lot out of me to realize what needed to be done, planning a memorial service that I never should've had to have planned in the first place, a death that wasn't meant to happen.

Kam was gone too soon, and I never got a chance to say goodbye.

My best friend was gone and I was left to mourn the loss of him. The memories we once shared, and the times we had. Were all left to fade into black without him around to share them with.

I lightly clear my throat, gazing around the crowded room of people, filling the service, who make their way down the aisle to their seats. A smile tugs at the corner of my lips as Otis makes his way up to the front of the room to a podium to speak.

Otis pulls at the collar of his black suit jacket, watching the nerves run right through him. He tries to smile for the crowd. But his emotions begin to break him in an uncontrollable manner.

"Thank you for coming today—" his voice stutters. He nods to himself, flipping open his notebook to start reading the speech he prepared. He stares out into the crowd to watch for my nod for him to continue on.

"Kam was one of my friends—and toward the end...he and I didn't see eye-to-eye. I regret that as I look back at it, because I didn't know the little time he had left—" his voice breaks, allowing a tear to fall down his cheek. "Kam was different...there was nobody quite like him—"

His break grows more into a sob, cutting off the words he can't bear to continue on with. He flips over his piece of paper, glancing over in my direction again with a shake of his head.

He couldn't do this.

Otis looks over his shoulder to the portrait of Kam that sat next to his cremains, filling the urn. Another tear falls. "I'm sorry—I can't do this..."

He rushes back to his seat, next to mine. I brush my hand along his shoulder for a moment of reassurance, as he pushes his notebook back into his pocket to begin sobbing even louder than before.

"You did great, Otis," I whispered softly, so only he could hear. "Kam would have loved it."

A soft nod lets out of Otis, pulling my hand back to brush it along the side of my dress pants. I stare forward to gather the context of the room, in what I hadn't observed before.

Many dark scarlet colored red roses and a soft shade of pink carnation scatter around where the urn was placed on a table. A portrait of Kam sat next to it, as well decorated with the lining of the many colorful shades of flowers.

Photo boards fill the surrounding areas around the room to show the life Kam had lived. To show where he was once happy, even if he didn't want to bear himself to show it to others. I knew his life had more that could be told, that pictures just couldn't show or even explain.

His life was a story in itself. Another chapter with another page turned. The words that were put together with an unexpected twist, I didn't even want to see coming. In the end, maybe it was all meant to have happened.

Kam's story was put to an end, much sooner than I would have liked. A closing of a page, an end of a chapter. Simply the end of an era. But in the end of it all, death is meant to happen. Death can proceed the things we never wanted to face.

The fact of life, that many could never seem to understand why things happen in life, in the way that they did.

Every action. Every thought. Every desire.

Why does it happen? Why did *this* have to happen?

Why did the killing of Kam have to happen?

My mind grows hazy, zoning out in the distance and lost in a thought I wanted to be lost in forever, until I found the answers to it. A smile tugs at my lips as I think back to the great memories I had with Kam.

I never wanted to forget them. Never wanted to forget him.

"Lipton–" a voice calls out from the front of the room. My attention quickly snaps out of my thought to dart over to the voice calling my name. The funeral director stands there, gesturing to the podium. "You may speak now if you'd still like to."

I nod, standing to my feet. I glance over to Otis with one last brush of my hand to his shoulder as I make my way up to the front of the room. I pull a piece of paper out of the inside lining of my black suit jacket to hold in my hands, staring out toward the crowd of people, who were filled with many emotions.

I clear my throat with a slight nod to myself. "I've known Kam for quite some time, and having been faced with the thought of losing him, hurt me a lot more than I want to realize at the moment. It still doesn't feel like he's gone, as his memories still live on. I still hear his voice. His soft laugh, and the ones we shared when we were together when he would come to support me in the times I needed him the most. Kam was always there."

There's a break in my voice with another clearing of my throat as I glance over in Otis' direction to watch his tearful eyes.

"Kam was my best friend–" my voice breaks, realizing the pain within it. "I never want to forget that and the times we shared. Every moment that was made. Every memory we shared. I never want to forget the friend I had, and still have living on in my heart."

My words prick tears in the corner of the crowd's eyes, thanking them softly as I make my way over to the urn. I press my hand gently against it, running the tip of my thumb back and forth. A tear runs down my cheek, being faced with the last moment I would ever get to share with Kam.

A moment I couldn't bear to see as our last.

"I'm sorry–you deserved better than what you had. Now you'll get the chance to have it. Just without us by your side. I already miss you–but this isn't goodbye," I softly whisper toward the urn. "I couldn't have asked for a better friend than you, Kam."

I pull my hand back slightly, lowering it down to my side. A sigh lets out of me, taking my seat next to Otis for the rest of the service to continue on as my mind drifts back into its endless thoughts.

This wasn't the end. Kam's life still had so much to live for. So much more story that could be told. I wouldn't allow this to be the death of him in my mind, faced with his death in real life. His thought would live on, only if I allowed it to.

The service commemorates in a soft tone of dismissal, watching everyone stand to their feet to make their way around the room, to either pay their respects or glance over the photo boards of the life Kam had.

I glance over my shoulder to face Otis. A smile making its attempt to pull at the corners of it, not baring to show my weakness of how much this hurt me to face head-on. My attention eases off of Otis with a soft nod in a way to tell him that he was going to be alright.

I gather my thoughts around the room, catching a glimpse of a tall, familiar figure filling the entryway of the room, who appeared to be passing off their condolences to Kam's parents. Standing in a well-pressed black suit, stood Coach Becker with a breaking smile.

It made no sense why he was here. He didn't know Kam like everyone else did.

My hand gently brushes along Otis' shoulder, pushing to make my way past him. "I'll be right back."

He nods as I begin to make my way down the aisle, filled with a crowd of people lining it. My eyes stay straight ahead, never straying away from Becker's appearance, as each step I take is another step closer to him.

Another step closer to wondering why he was here.

But by the time I got through the crowd of people, it appeared to be too late. The figure of Becker that once filled the doorway was no more. He had faded into nothing, as if he had become a lurking presence just to fill my mind in the meantime with everything that was truly going on, that I didn't want to face.

I stare over the room, lost in a brand new thought. The figure of him became a void that I couldn't seem to understand. The thought of the one thing I began to wonder in the back of my mind.

To look at things to question if you really know a person for who they really are, or if everything you were taught to learn growing up was all just a big misunderstanding for who a person really is deep down at the end of the day.

The things you grow to trust, would become the things that would break you in the end. The thoughts you never wanted to face. The ones you never wanted to relive, would only be the ones you could never seem to be able to escape at the end of it all.

Acknowledgments

Well, here we are, the acknowledgment page of my debut novel. In all the time, the years of craftsmanship, it has taken me to build this project up from nothing into something I never imagined I'd be making it to this page of the book.

This project, *Killing Kam*, has become something I will hold dear and close to my heart for years to come for many different reasons. When the idea of this novel came to me, I was living in my lowest and uncertain times of my life. I had just dropped out of college, clueless of what I wanted to do with my life, and I emotionally had a lot going on that I was unsure of how to deal with at the time.

But when the idea of *Killing Kam* came to be one day, I knew I had to work with the idea to go into it with a goal I've always had and an ending that I knew needed to be told in some sort of way.

I was going to write and publish a book, despite what everyone had told me growing up.

For years, I have spent my life behind a notebook with a pen in hand, born to make a vision come to life. To be able to form many different stories to share when the time is right and you're able to believe in yourself, for what your heart has always been telling you.

There are many things in life that you could look back on and wish to have changed to have gotten yourself to a certain point. This story isn't something I would have wished to have done differently or wanted to change, as I believe it was all meant to have happened for a reason. A story to be told at the right time.

And that's exactly what this story is meant to tell. The past, present, and future are all unfolding at your grasp. Your control in the way you want it to happen. You just have to reach out and make it yours.

Well I could go on for pages, ranting about other things than what we're actually here for. This is the acknowledgement page after all, so I think it's fair to get to the point of acknowledging some people. That's only fair, right?

I would first like to thank my younger self, who had a vision and a dream she felt was worth chasing, despite how many people told her that she couldn't do it. A dream people thought wasn't worth the time for an opportunity they didn't think she'd have a chance at achieving.

From the age of twelve, she never gave up. She kept working harder at each book she wrote, she'd work even harder on the next to make sure it was better than the last. Until she found and wrote the right words for the one she felt it was worth sharing.

But no matter how many people told her, she couldn't do it. She needed to prove them wrong. And look at her now, she wrote and published a book—didn't she?

Moving onward with the list of acknowledgements, I would like to thank my family. Especially my grandma in particular, who would sit down with me after I had written a few chapters. She would take the time to read it over and tell me what she thought, and even fix some of the mistakes.

I would also love to thank all of the authors, who have helped me get here, who I've had the chance of talking to over the course of the last year. If that was at a book signing or even a simple question on a social media platform, who all started on the same independent publishing journey.

I would love to thank author Lauren Roberts (*Powerless*) who helped me the most when it came to the book publishing world. If that meant having to stay after a signing to talk to me, even helping me learn how to copyright, basically anything I had a question on, you were there to be able to answer it and I thank you, Lauren for that.

But with all this being said, and all the help and thanks I can give. Things have to come to an end at some point. No matter if you flip the page over and it's blank, this story isn't quite over yet. And I hope you will allow me to continue doing what I love, putting words onto paper to build a story because there's still more to be told. I'll promise you that.

With much love, *xoxo Gabs.*

About The Author

Gabrielle Jones was born and raised in a small town in Michigan her whole life, so she is no stranger to the cold weather. She enjoys spending most of her time writing when she has the chance, mostly in the middle of the night when she should be sleeping. She enjoys being able to bring a story to life, being able to capture a story that could easily be told and something that many can relate to at some point in their lives. When Gabrielle isn't writing either a romance or thriller, she enjoys spending her time with friends or even making a playlist of songs to match her next novel. To stay connected with her, follow her on socials everywhere at Gabriellejonesauthor.

www.ingramcontent.com/pod-product-compliance
Lightning Source LLC
Chambersburg PA
CBHW050007120726
47903CB00006B/1668